Radharao F. Gracias
AUTHOR

A Shortcut to Tipperary
(From Goa)

A Novel

Radharao F. Gracias

A Shortcut to Tipperary
(From Goa)

© **Radharao F. Gracias**

First Edition: 2022

© **Published by**

BROADWAY
PUBLISHING HOUSE

SIGNATURE STORE:
1st Floor, Ashirwad Bldg., Near Caculo Island, 18th June Road, Panjim-Goa.
Tel: 2420677, 6647037, 6647038, Fax: 6647038
Email: *bbcbooks@rediffmail.com info@booksingoa.com*
Website: *www.booksingoa.com*

Edited by Alexandre Barbosa Moniz

Cover & Illustrations by Norman Tagore

ISBN NO.: 978-93-84298-99-9

Printed by Impressions, Belgaum

To

José Francisco Aniceto Lusitano Socrates do Menino Jesus
Gracias

Foreword

Radharao Gracias known all over Goa and wherever Goans abound, is famous for being a formidable lawyer with a sharp, incisive mind. A Shortcut to Tipperary his debut novel demonstrates that he has interests that go far beyond law. The title is certainly intriguing and we don't get our answers till we near the end.

The first of 34 short chapters is titled The Dream and though it's the longest, it gives the reader no hint of where the novel is going. The novel opens and ends too with a dream sequence take-off from Paulo Coelho's The Alchemist. We meet the protagonist Ismael in the metropolis of Bombay. Though fate has been cruel to the young orphan, it hasn't embittered him. His humanity is intact. As he empathises with a blind vagabond begging for alms on the roadside, Ismael learns that he is a victim of a ruthless syndicate which creates and exploits beggars. Using the technique of Magical Realism the genre of blending fact and fantasy, made famous by the Nobel-winning Colombian novelist Gabriel Garcia Marquez, the author has the blind beggar Alberto cured of his blindness and the duo acquiring a respectable hoard of money. They team up and flee from the syndicate in Bombay and after some adventures and diversions, they land in Goa. This is where the real action begins.

The author uses the novel and his principal characters to enlighten us with his own truly encyclopaedic knowledge of the local flora and fauna, especially the avifauna, which arguably equals that of a trained ornithologist. His evocative descriptions of nature remind me of the naturalist Gerald Durrel in *My Family and* Other Animals. In the bargain, the reader is also given a more than authentic glimpse of life in a typical predominantly

Catholic village of South Goa, of the 1960s & 70s. The novel is enhanced by excellent illustrations.

Radharao weaves a compelling, sometimes improbable, but always captivating tale that holds us in thrall as we meet the staples of Goan village life - Church, School, Beach, Fishermen, Farmers and the ubiquitous Taverna. Some of the places and characters that people the novel, are taken from real life – names and all! We also get a glimpse of how the criminal justice system works. Despite being a lawyer, his personal scepticism of the law being able to deliver justice comes through clearly.

Mercifully, he touches only peripherally, upon Goa's staple topics of politics and corruption. Instead, he takes us back into history, enlightening us about the hundreds of non-combatant Goan war casualties aboard passenger ships converted overnight into Allied troop carriers in World War Two. We learn about the ingenious *Kudd* or Village Club system of a home away from home for Goans temporarily in Bombay, instituted by the early Goan seafarers and the simple but strict rules they abide by.

We expect something connected with law from a lawyer and we are not disappointed as the Chapter Evidence and Arguments gives the layman a glimpse into how a civil case proceeds. We also learn that not all talk about judicial bribery is true. But in four chapters beginning with The Countermanding, we are given a sometimes hilarious take on the famous Poll Countermanding Case which, after dragging on and wasting the resources of the State for over two decades, only proved that sometimes the law is indeed an ass!

The novel lets us into simple but ingenious local secrets of catching birds and trapping wild boars, the lore of the fishermen and even a macabre score-settling vendetta, that has us applauding rather than condemning the perpetrator!

We are also reminded about the many positive legacies of Portuguese rule – exotic plants like the Cashew, Potato, Chilly and others transported by them from South America, as also the art of distillation and bread-making.

The institution of a State-appointed Regedor or village head, during Portuguese rule, who settled most village problems without burdening the judicial system, is replaced in the novel by The Bhatkar. The Landlord was an unelected, un-appointed, but much-respected, benevolent, upright man who was a byword for kindness and generosity and dispensed common-sense justice which was acceptable to all the parties.

It is apparent that the author besides being a prodigious reader has also kept abreast of musical trends and has certainly done a lot of research, as we see in the chapter Bob Marley. Good lawyer that he is, he convinces us (tongue firmly in cheek!) that Bob in his reggae hit, actually sang a line in Konkani!

The last chapters take heart-stopping turns. But The Toast delivered by The Bhatkar is truly the epitome of an excellent toast, eerily reminiscent of toasts raised by that excellent toastmaster Radharao Gracias!

What comes through is an unapologetic pride in his Goenkarponn and he sets, the record straight on the largely unsung contribution of the Goan Catholic to the nation. He's not happy that hundreds of thousands of Goans are forced to leave behind a land they love so much and even to acquire foreign nationality as Goa cannot provide jobs for her sons, but he hopefully rationalises that they will come back at least occasionally to renew their ties with their motherland.

The novel *A Shortcut to Tipperary* is a meticulously crafted, delightful, morality play that heralds the arrival of an extremely talented, insightful writer on the English fiction scene and has readers anticipating a speedy sequel.

Xavier Cota

Acknowledgements

As my first book goes into print I have to acknowledge the role played by so many individuals, but for whom you would not be reading the book.

The one topping the list is my wife, to whom I dictated most of the manuscript over innumerable sittings, at all times of day and night. She is, I suppose that rare wife who allowed herself to be dictated to by her husband and without protest too! And my daughter Sukriti (who is at the beginning of a career in writing) whose suggestions have also gone into the book.

My sincere thanks are to:

The editor Alexandre Barbosa Moniz for meticulously combing through the text and streamlining it.

The artist Norman Tagore for the cover and the illustrations

My neighbor down the road, Xavier Cota who has carefully sifted through the text and made valuable suggestions and written the Foreword.

The publisher Ms Broadway Publishing House who gracefully offered to publish my book.

The printer Rama Harmalkar for his diligent work.

The hundreds of readers of my column in the newspapers and in the electronic media who have constantly urged me to write a book.

The general reader, who I hope and trust, will find the book worthwhile.

And all those others who helped make this book a reality and whose names I may have missed out.

Index

Chapter 1

Tħe Dream

"Look," I hear a voice speak to me. "I did not ignore my dream. I followed it".

I find it difficult to comprehend. I wake up. I cannot fathom anything. I try to forget it, as I do with most of my other dreams, as just another dream. But it repeats, night after night. And I wake up before the dream is complete but each time the dream lasts just a little longer. I can see a young shepherd with brown hair and brown eyes. He is trying to convey a message. Then one night I do not wake up. I experience the dream fully as if it is a movie. I can gather that the shepherd gives up his occupation and goes on a journey from Andalucia in Spain through North Africa to Egypt. His journey is full of hazards. He undergoes Odysseus-like trials before his destiny is fulfilled. He meets strangers, is robbed of his money, is witness to an alchemist convert lead into gold, falls in love, and is beaten almost to death. But in the end through suffering and pain he is fulfilled. The dream is clear and real.

At the end he commands, "Go find your destiny; find your personal legend.

"What use is life if you do not fulfil your destiny? Go, find your legend. Remember, strange, unexpected and unbelievable events will cross your path along the journey. But when opportunity knocks, do not hesitate. The road ahead may be paved with pain and suffering. Eventually the dark clouds will move away. And the sun will rise, spreading warmth and cheer. You will be fulfilled."

I wake up in a sweat. And I cannot sleep again.

I continue to toss in bed, restive and a little disoriented. As I see sunlight creep in through the gap in the window I get out of bed feeling unusually hungry and drowsy. I light a fire, brew coffee brush my teeth and have a wash. After a steaming cup of coffee I begin my walk to the church. The pavements are still free of crowds. The drowsy feeling returns and my eyes cloud up. I step into a wayside kiosk and order a soda. The bottle is opened and the cap flies in a parabola and lands in my pocket. I take the bottle, splash some soda on my face, drink a little and splash more on my face. I repeat the process until the bottle is empty, drop the change returned by the kiosk owner into my pocket, rest for about five minutes on the stool by the side of the kiosk and forget the bottle cap, still in my pocket. Fully recovered I resume my walk to church.

The sun is up as a few early risers begin to crowd the pavement. As I proceed, I see in the distance, the familiar silhouette of the sausage tree rising high and spreading wide, its drooping branches full of fruit. The old blind beggar, with an Afonso de Albuquerque beard and a Mahatma Gandhi hairline, squats under the tree muttering something incoherent and stretching his hand out with his bowl, which he knocks against the pavement to attract attention. I put my hand in my pocket and drop a coin only to realise from the feel of its crimped edges that I have dropped the bottle cap instead. I look down only to see a coin in the bowl. I recheck my pocket. No bottle cap in it.

But the two twenty-five paise coins returned by the soda seller still jingle in my pocket.

As I proceed ahead I am confused. The confusion remains and I hardly follow the Mass. On my way back, I decide to investigate. I empty my pocket of all change and fill it with a few bottle caps picked up from the roadside. The beggar is by now a little quiescent. I take a bottle cap out of my pocket, and consciously drop it. And I witness the miracle. The cap of a Coca Cola bottle has turned into a two rupee coin. I look carefully around and drop the remaining caps which too become coins. I look in disbelief, but avoid drawing attention. If someone does notice, the implications could be unpredictable for both of us.

I spend a sleepless night unable to understand the day's happenings. The next day as I proceed to work, I collect a few more caps. The beggar's bowl turns them into coins. Unbelievable! So I keep the knowledge of the occurrence to myself. No one has witnessed this alchemy. Actually, I am afraid that if someone does witness the transformation it may come to an end, so I am particularly stealthy.

I keep dropping bottle caps in the bowl for maybe two years or longer. As I think it over I begin to wonder why must only the beggar benefit from the largesse? Why must I also not partake of the coins from the bowl? So one day, I bend low before dropping the caps and in the same motion flip a coin or two. My hand only holds caps. I drop them back and they revert to coins. I vow in anger never to drop any more caps. Why must I keep dropping coins without any benefit to me?

The next day as I walk past without dropping any bottle caps into the bowl, the beggar looks at me with unseeing eyes and he strains his neck to follow me until I am way past him. The following days I keep passing by and his sightless eyes follow me. He knocks his bowl on the pavement with greater vigour. I think I am imagining things.

Sunday Mass weeks later and the reading is the **Gospel of**

Luke Chapter 10 :

'Behold, a certain lawyer stood up and tested him, saying, "Teacher, what shall I do to inherit eternal life?"

He said to him, "What is written in the law? How do you read it?"

He answered, "You shall love the Lord your God with all your heart, with all your soul, with all your strength, and with all your mind; and your neighbour as yourself."

He said to him, "You have answered correctly. Do this, and you will live."

But he, desiring to justify himself, asked Jesus, "Who is my neighbour?"

—Luke 10:25–29,

Jesus replies with a story:

Jesus answered, "A certain man was going down from Jerusalem to Jericho, and he fell among robbers, who both stripped him and beat him, and departed, leaving him half dead. By chance a certain priest was going down that way. When he saw him, he passed by on the other side. In the same way a Levite also, when he came to the place, and saw him, passed by on the other side. But a certain Samaritan, as he travelled, came where he was. When he saw him, he was moved with compassion, came to him, and bound up his wounds, pouring on oil and wine. He set him on his own animal, and brought him to an inn, and took care of him. On the next day, when he departed, he took out two denarii, gave them to the host, and said to him, 'Take care of him. Whatever you spend beyond that, I will repay you when I return.' Now which of these three do you think seemed to be a neighbour to him who fell among the robbers?"

He said, "He who showed mercy on him."

Then Jesus said to him, "Go and do likewise".'

The priest ends the homily with the observation "Any good that you can do must be done without expectation of anything in return."

And that immediately strikes a chord. Have I done right?

And do I lose anything by merely dropping bottle caps? Must I not resume dropping the caps? The answer presents itself. I begin to collect and drop bottle caps again.

The process goes on for weeks, months, a year and beyond, turning bottle caps into coins until it is time for me to take a few days off to go for a trip with friends to Mahabaleshwar. Even here, the beggar continues to hover in my mind. I just cannot forget him.

I return after a week and as usual drop a few caps into the bowl. Suddenly there is a painful cry as the beggar curses me for playing the fool by dropping bottle caps instead of coins. I look back to find no coins but bottle caps in the bowl. And a different beggar this time. My old friend is not there. In fact, the practice of dropping bottle caps had become so mechanical that I sometimes did not even glance at the beggar.

I double back a few steps, I rectify the situation, drop a coin in the bowl and retrieve the caps to the beggar's delight. He is unable to tell me anything about the previous occupant of the place under the tree. He does not know or pretends not to know anything at all.

The little shop next door too knows nothing about him. However, I learn that there are several syndicates that have divided the turf between them. This area is controlled by a Chembur-based group which brings the beggars early in the morning before the shops open and place them at their selected spots. They are provided meals in the afternoon and late evening after rush hour are taken back to their resting places. The process is repeated daily. I was disturbed by the fact that all my caps turned into coins had gone to the syndicate and my efforts for the beggar were in vain.

I get curious to trace my beggar particularly so because the phenomenon of transformation of coins failed with the changed beggar. After all have I not dropped bottle caps worth thousands of rupees in his bowl? And have I not developed a bond with him? Have I not seen the magical transformation of bottle caps into coins? Why must the alchemy stop with a different beggar? I am intrigued.The same evening I borrow a scooter from a friend, ride and park some distance from the tree. Late in the evening, a taxi comes and the beggar goes in. I follow the taxi which picks up several other beggars from different spots. The taxi then drives to Chembur and drops all of them at a slum. From a distance I can see all types of beggars – blind, lame and decrepit – enter a lane and disappear into several shack-type structures helped by attendants, where help is needed.

I bide my time and the following Sunday before lunch, when the beggars are at rest, I take a bus and make my way into the slums. And find my man squatting by the pavement in the shade of a tree.

I walk towards him, he is alert and smiles at me and shouts out a hello. I thought it was a general greeting. But no, he says:

"I've been missing you."

"How do you know who I am?"

"I do not know who you are. But I can recognise your approach from your footsteps when you are a long way off, followed by the sound of coins dropped in my bowl. I do not need to see you to recognise you."

I hug him at his response. He holds me tight and then shrieks out with an expression of pain and joy at the same time.

"Can you see that I can see?" says he.

His eyesight is restored and he is ecstatic beyond words. It is the second miracle.

As he walks into what he calls his home, he invites me in. All I see is a hovel with sack cloth for walls and a low roof of zinc sheets resting on flimsy poles. A mat is spread on the floor and except for a large tin trunk there is no other item of furniture. He invites me to sit on the trunk. He gets busy searching for something. He seems not to find what he is looking for and is visibly distraught as he stomps around the little room perhaps not more than six yards square. After some time he looks at me and says,

"It is gone.Where could it go?"

I do not understand what he is looking for until he tells me. As he cries out in agony, I get an idea. I request him to quieten down. I take a handkerchief from my pocket and tie it around his eyes restoring the blind state in which he has lived for years. Soon his hands trace the hollow in the floor in the corner. He digs out two rather heavy cloth bundles, as can be determined from the effort he puts in to lift each. He was so accustomed to being blind that restoration of sight had actually blinded him!

"Let's go before the syndicate finds out. I could be blinded again. No time to waste," he orders.

He puts everything into the trunk and locks it with a key from his trouser pocket. He catches the handle on one side while I hold the other. A yellow and black taxi passing by is hailed. The trunk fits into the boot with great difficulty. Both of us fit in the rear, with greater ease.

"Let's go to VT," says the old man as the taxi drives off.

"We are going to Goa," asserts the old man

"Not I," is my response.

"What do you mean? You and I are part of a divine plan that has just been set off. Have you not witnessed a miracle? Both of us have to work in tandem. You know it. You have no right to abandon it."

"But I cannot simply run away just like that" I say. "Because, I have commitments at my work place."

"Forget the commitments. There is something supernatural about what has happened and you cannot decamp. We have to work together. And what do I do with all this money? It belongs more to you. I am satisfied with the restoration of my sight. You have a greater commitment to a greater but unseen force."

But how can I just abandon Bombay and run away to a place of which I know nothing? My mind is in a tizzy. Should I risk the unknown?

I vividly recall the Spanish shepherd and his plea to find my personal legend. I see before my very eyes the alchemist turning lead into gold for the shepherd boy in the dream. And in real life, I have witnessed bottle caps turning into coins for the beggar. And a blind man's sight restored. Is it the same force at work? Is it not a compelling parallel? Is this the journey that the shepherd has urged me to take? Do I hear opportunity knock? Should I not give it a try?

He fixes me with the stare of his restored eyes. I have to agree. I direct the taxi to the Flora Fountain area, to the bookshop where I work, only to remember that being a Sunday the place is closed. Thus the taxi is redirected to Andheri to a room I share with a friend. Fortunately my friend is relaxing at home having returned from a game of football. The old man looks frightened and in a hurry to leave. I persuade him to relax, have a bath, change his clothes. After lunch the old man falls asleep in my bed. I do not disturb him. By the time he wakes up it is quite late. I write a quick note of leave of absence explaining the urgency and request my friend to deliver it to my workplace on the morrow. I pack the necessary items in my suitcase and take leave of my friend.

Despite being a Sunday the traffic is quite heavy. A little more than half an hour later, we can see the outline of Victoria Terminus looming ahead in the semi darkness, elegant, but incongruous in its setting and by far the most magnificent of that era of railway stations, in the country. Completed in the year 1887, as a plaque indicates, it is the hub of rail traffic in the acknowledged commercial capital of the country.

We step in and immediately move from colonial era and hopefully into modern and free India. Madding crowds push and pull in every direction. It is drummed into us in school that the British had bled India over centuries of its rule. Inside, I can see that freedom has made no difference. The pristine walls of the gothic edifice show signs of bleeding from every nook and corner; a closer look indicates it is betel spit. And fresh too.

The train to Goa, scheduled for the evening has been cancelled. We find ourselves in a soup. Upon hectic inquiries we are informed that there may be no trains to Goa for a week or more as major repairs to the railway line have been necessitated. The Station Master is unable to provide further details except to say that the trains will resume as soon as possible. Typical official jargon, which as always, is neither here nor there.

"The syndicate is ubiquitous. It has its tentacles everywhere. I cannot fall into their hands again," murmurs the now perspiring beggar.

"I have to be out of Bombay somehow. And quickly too. I am their prized beggar. They will not let me go if they can help it. Let's go to Bangalore or Hyderabad from where we can later make it to Goa," he decides.

I check at the ticket counter. A train to Hyderabad is due in an hour from where we can proceed to Londa via Hubli which route is operational. We buy tickets. My companion continues to perspire and looks uneasy.

We rush in as the train arrives. We have to overcome the usual pushing and shoving from all sides before we gain entry. We have no reservations but manage to get good seats opposite each other by the window. As the train starts moving it can be seen that a large number of seats are empty even in the general compartment. But not for long as after a few more stations, passengers barge in and the feeling of space is lost.

The train leaves the city and in about an hour reaches Thane. After a long wait, the journey resumes over a dark unlighted but level countryside until we reach Bhor Ghat. The climb is slow, labourious and grueling as the train winds its way through tunnel after tunnel. I stop counting the number after ten. The train halts at Khandala. The station is dimly lit and a few passengers come in before the train rolls out.We begin talking as sleep does not seem to come to either of us.

"Were you blind from birth? Or did you go blind at a later

stage?"

"I was perfectly normal well into my early twenties. And I could see as well as anyone."

"And what were you doing for a living?"

"I was trying to find a short cut to Tipperary," he says with a smile.

"Obviously you did not find it, but tell me what instrument were you playing?"

He looks at me in disbelief. "But how did you guess I was into music?"

"Well, who else but a musician will try to find a short cut to Tipperary?" was my retort.

"Smart of you," says he.

The old man bends under the seat and pulls out the trunk and carefully takes out something wrapped in cloth from it. After unwrapping it he takes it to his mouth and begins to blow. It is a trumpet.To my astonishment after a few tentative notes, he began to play, "It's a Long Way to Tipperary".

I tap his knee and tell him to halt for a moment. Other passengers look on. As he resumes playing I sing the lyrics. This time it's his turn to be astonished:

Up to mighty London came
An Irish lad one day,
All the streets were paved with gold,
So everyone was gay!
Singing songs of Piccadilly,
Strand, and Leicester Square,
Til Paddy got excited and
He shouted to them there:
It's a long way to Tipperary,
It's a long way to go.
It's a long way to Tipperary
To the sweetest girl I know!
Goodbye Piccadilly,
Farewell Leicester Square!

It's a long long way to Tipperary,
But my heart's right there........

As abruptly as he had begun, he stops. But I continue to sing not having expected the interruption. I look at him and tears drop from his eyes as he gets emotional.

"What happened?"

"It was on this note that the bomb hit my ship HMT Rohna. It was 26th of November 1943. We were in the Mediterranean Sea," he pauses.

He seems to have fallen into a stupor. I have to shake him up a bit. He returns to earth drinks a little water from the bottle he's carrying and resumes the narration.

"Let me begin from the beginning. My name is Alberto. I was born in Bombay and lived with my mother, father and sister in a room at Mahim. But as the room was too small, after I grew up, I found a place to live in our village club located in Jer Mahal Building, Dhobitalao. My father too was a member of the club. I soon found work as a kitchen helper in the Taj, but I did not have my heart in it. I would have preferred to work as a musician as I was quite facile with the trumpet. But as with other Goans, my long time dream was to work on the ship.

"After a few months, luck smiled, as a relative who worked for British India Steam Navigation Company returned from a voyage and came over to the club. Before returning to Goa he took me to his shipping company office and requested another Goan working there to recruit me.

"Thus promptly, by the age of twenty-one, I was on the SS Rajula as a General Seaman. Life on the ship was hectic and tiresome but I had no complaints. I was aware that as a new recruit I would be exploited by senior staff. I was prepared for it."

At this point the train begins to slow down and comes to a halt. The signal is not aligned for the train to enter the station. There is shouting and noisy scenes as some passengers de-board the train as they are nearer home than they would be from the station. After calm returns, Alberto resumes.

"The SS Rajula overawed me, the ship being huge, much beyond what I had expected it would be. The first trips were between Madras and Singapore and other ports in Malaya It was hard, hectic work but enjoyable. The passengers were poor and spoke so many languages, none of which were intelligible to me. The ship could accommodate some five thousand passengers. My postings rotated between SS Rajula and SS Rohna, both having been launched around the same time.

"Inevitably and in short order came the dreaded requisition. Both the ships were drafted as troop ships to enhance the war effort. The SS Rohna thus became HMT Rohna. The crewmen were given the option of disembarking and returning home or continuing to work at double the salaries. I opted to continue, carried by my youthful exuberance and inherent nature to court danger and the opportunity to make quick money."

Another interruption, as the train resumes the journey and soon halts at a decrepit but crowded little station. The railway station scene by now familiar, repeats itself. Pretty difficult to make conversation in the hustle and bustle. A long whistle signals that the train is about to move.

Alberto resumes:

"When the war broke out I was on HMT Rohna and continued to be on that ship. In December, 1941, we travelled from Bombay to Marseille and then for a few months plied between Haifa in Palestine and Marseille. The ship continued to traverse the Indian Ocean for the next two years and transported troops during the Anglo-Iraqi war. I liked the challenge so I opted out of regular leave. Better to earn as much as possible in a short period and then return and settle back in my village."

"However, things turned for the worse after Japan invaded Malaya. We rescued people from Singapore before the Japanese took over the city. For the remainder of the year 1942, the Rohna criss-crossed the Arabian Sea moving between India and West Asia. When the ship had docked in Bombay I did go on shore leave on a few occasions, met my parents and sister. There were food shortages and I managed to take some essentials from the ship and deliver to them. Later in the year 1943, the ship sailed to the Mediterranean to carry troops in the North African campaign."

"The ship after being drafted had retained the band as the troops needed entertainment. As it happened, on one occasion the trumpeter of the band took seriously ill and could not play as he had pneumonia and was discharged from his duties. The next morning I took my own trumpet which I always carried with me, went to the bandmaster and began to play. He was wonderstruck that an Indian seaman could play a western instrument and immediately condescended to give me a trial.

"The same night, as the band played, the troops were quite pleased with my control on the instrument and my knowledge of music. I received a standing ovation with a demand from the recruits to the bandmaster that I must continue to play in the band which was immediately conceded. Actually, there was no choice as another trumpeter could not be easily sourced in those difficult days. And thus, from a deckhand I became a band man. My joy knew no bounds as my ambition to be a musician and a seaman were both fulfilled in one stroke. You see the Captain of the ship was an Irisman and a veteran of the First World War. The Tipperary song was quite popular then. He loved it and frequently insisted that it be played.

"On 25th November 1943, we left Oran in Algeria carrying American troops. And there was a contingent of Asian crew too which the British classified as a lascars. We were sailing quite close to the coast. I remember the date because it is the same date on which Afonso de Albuquerque liberated Goa from Idalcao at the invitation of local leaders Thimaya Nayak from Honavar and Mhal Poi, from Verna, as we learnt in school. The next day a formation of Luftwaffe bombers attacked the ship. We survived the first wave. Several casualties were inflicted on the Germans by our armed escort. I saw at least one German bomber crash into the sea. We believed that the Germans had given up and that we had survived unscathed. The captain ordered the band to play, to release the tension and by way of a celebration. It was about five pm. As we were playing, the second wave of bombers flew in and unknown to us a bomb hit the ship on the portside with devastating effect. Explosions started a massive fire and sent debris flying, knocked out the lights and water supply. Soon it was clear that the ship would sink. Chaos ruled as some of the lascars lowered lifeboats and fled the sinking ship without helping launch the other boats or assisting in the rescue. My face was burnt but I could still see somewhat."

The narration stops. He gets emotional and in pain as he relives the tragic moment. He remains mum for a long time as the train keeps pushing. I do not disturb him. After an interminable silence he returns to the present and resumes the narrative.

"The whole ship then caught fire in several places and the survivors tried desperately to put them off. But the fires were too big and the damage too great. The ships in the convoy began to rescue the survivors. The more serious ones were lifted first. I had burns all over my body and could hardly see anything. The ship sank, within a short time.

"The rescue went on for the whole night even after the ship had sunk, and people, some with serious injuries were rescued.

"I found myself drifting in and out of consciousness. When I finally regained my senses, I was on a bed in an overcrowded hospital. Here, there was relative safety from German bombers but there was scarcity of medicines. I know not what happened to the crew and the troops. But, throughout my ordeal, my trumpet remained with me. I understand that I was holding it tight when I was rescued. And the hospital kept it on my bed as I was recovering as the doctors believed it may speed up my recovery. And it has remained with me as my only link with the past.

"I had sufficiently recovered by the end of two months, when I with other Indians was put on board the ship to India.

We arrived in Bombay. But throughout this ordeal I was afraid that another German raid may attack us anytime. I was then admitted to KEM Hospital, which after a few days insisted on my discharge and return as an outpatient; I had nowhere to go. So I remained hanging around in the corridors of the hospital for a a few days. By this time I could see quite well with my right eye, but the damage to my left eye was a little more severe. Doctors advised that my normal sight would be restored with medication and rest.

"Patients and their relatives were coming to the hospital throughout my stay there. But I had no visitors. I managed to make friends with one Inacio D'Melo, who I used to see regularly at the hospital. He informed me that he was a social worker who would come to take care of unattended patients. I explained my plight to him. He readily agreed to take me and place me with some persons who would help me. Being a Goan, like me, I implicitly trusted him.

"So, I accompanied him to his room, where I stayed with him for a night. The next day some other social workers came over and took me in their care. I was assured that I would be helped to recover fully from my injuries and then put in touch with my family. They brought some person identified as an ophthalmologist who prescribed medication for the eyes. After a few days my eyesight worsened and by the following week I became totally blind. The social workers then took me with them, starved me for a few days, beat me up and forced me to beg. The only concession made was to permit me to retain my trumpet. It took me quite some time to understand that this was a racket which controlled beggars in the city and preyed on hapless patients. I had earlier heard about it. Inacio was their front man. Now, I often wonder whether his name was actually Inacio or that was a false name under which he carried out his nefarious activities.

"I have his entire features and voice fixated in my mind. For years, I have dreamed of catching him and bringing him to justice for ruining my life after I had survived the bombing. I have had to endure so much. He destroyed my life. I am sure if I hear him anywhere I will recognize him. And I will give him the treatment he deserves."

Once again he falls silent for a long time and looks lost and remote.

"The syndicate is terrible and unforgiving. I am given a weekly target to meet and if I do not collect that much, I am deprived of meals and even beaten up. I devised a strategy where any daily collection above the target limit is saved by me, a part buried under the tree and a part taken home. Whenever the collections are less than the target which was rarely the case, after you came in the picture, I would retrieve some coins from my hidden hoard, to make up the deficit. As charity was believed to be greater among those going to or returning from Mass, I had to beg on Sunday mornings too; the spot allotted to me was on the way to a church.

"My earnings increased manifold, after you came. Sometimes you alone contributed more than a normal day's earnings. I realised from the beginning that if my collection increases regularly then my limit may also get raised. Thus, most of what you dropped, came to be saved. And I did not know how long your blessings would continue. You did stop dropping in my bowl for about a month. I could hear you walk past me without dropping. And that hurt. You then resumed your charity. And was I glad. But I did show the daily earnings a little above the target to keep the syndicate happy. I was even pointed out as an example to the others."

"Tell me," he says. "How did you learn the Tipperary song?"

It is now my turn to detail my life. "I used to live in Byculla, on a footpath room slightly larger than the room in which I found you. My mother, my father and I. My father was a daily wage earner. My mother stayed at home. And then it happened. The riots. Hindu against Muslim. Muslim against Hindu. Nothing mattered. Not friendship not neighbourliness. Only religion.

"The crowd came howling in. I must have been three or four years old. Blood flowed in the streets and by the time it was over my father lay dead. Seeing the mayhem, I ran away and wandered aimlessly. I was picked up by someone and deposited with the nuns at Regina Pacis Convent opposite the Police Station at Byculla. The convent had become a virtual refugee centre for the homeless and the wounded. The nuns worked beyond the call of duty to provide succour to the unfortunates.

"After a few weeks, I was transferred to St. Stanislaus School at Bandra where the Jesuits had a boarding house for orphans. I grew up in the boarding house.

"I cried for days for my parents and particularly for my mother, being very attached to her. My father would be at home only at night and would be gone before I woke up. But he was a good man and he loved me. As I grew up, I did travel to the slum where I was born and made inquiries. The old slum has been rebuilt but with new occupants. None of the previous residents lived there anymore and none of the present knew my parents or pretended not to know them. Gradually I got the past out of my mind and adjusted to the realities of life. My name is Ismael. My father was Muslim, I understand. I was later baptised but my original name was retained as it was common to both Islam and Christianity."

Alberto looks at me and questions, "Are you certain?"

"Absolutely."

"How so?"

"I can prove it to you right now but not in a public place like the train."

"Why not?"

"Because, I will have to drop my trousers."

For the first time I hear Alberto laugh loud and clear.

"I believe my father was slaughtered after a similar verification". The laughter stops immediately.

"Well our music master was Fr. O'Brien a priest from Ireland. He was my godfather and was quite fond of me. It was his favourite song and he made me sing it constantly until I attained near perfection. I would frequently sing it to him.

"I was fortunate to have Fr. O'Brien as my mentor. He became my father and mother. He guided me in everything I did. After SSCE, because of my love for books, he encouraged me to go for a diploma in Library Science and secured admission for me at St Xavier's College Bombay. I put my days there, to optimum use and must have read more books then I had ever imagined I would.

"Fr. O'Brien loved the wilds and would spend his spare time in the wilderness that hugs the Bandra coast, with his binoculars identifying birds. I kept him company and developed an interest in birds. He was a member of the Bombay Natural History Society and had several books on birds and wildlife, an encyclopaedia and others. When he finally left for his homeland, he gifted his binoculars and all his books to me. And assured me that he will try to get me a visa to work in Ireland. He was confident he would be able to get me employed in any of the Church-run institutions of which there were plenty in that country. And for the last one year since he left I have scoured the same places he did, knowing for sure that he's doing his best to take me to his country.

Chapter 2

The Train Accident

The train speeds along in the darkness and makes several brief halts. It halts for a long time at Hyderabad. We take another train to Londa. After a few hours the train reduces speed to walking pace. And unexpectedly the couple sitting on the opposite seat with a boy not older than me between them bursts out crying and lamenting. It is early morning on a clear and bright day. The train halts as it has not received the signal to enter the station. Mangled compartments of a derailed train are lying in disarray alongside the track. The entire coach wakes up. The lamentation goes on and on rising to a crescendo coming down and rising again. All three appear to be totally in pain and suffering but it is difficult to discern what exactly the trouble is. After some time, one young man walks to them and shouts at them to keep quiet as everybody is being disturbed. The admonition has the opposite effect. The woman in particular starts wailing like a banshee and simply refuses to quieten down.

Alberto in desperation walks over, taps her softly on her back and asks kindly, what her troubles are. She soon calms down and begins her narration.

"My son Ajay had been proceeding to Bangalore looking for a job after he could not secure employment at Hyderabad. He was a bright boy and was matric passed, second class. We had scrounged from every source to educate him and we were confident that he would help us improve our lives and also help this younger brother further his studies. And my son, the jewel of our lives died right here, when the train crashed killing many people. He died here. He was in one of those derailed compartments we have just seen. My young son's life was nipped before he could bloom.

"We are poor, very poor. We have had to borrow money even to travel here. I do not know what will happen to us. Even the gods have forsaken us. Our only son who could have brought sunshine in our lives has been taken away. My son here is diabetic and suffers from many attendant ailments and Ajay was our only hope. Oh God why have you done this to us? Why do you not have mercy even on these poor creatures?" she demands.

"I can see nothing but darkness ahead," sobs her husband.

"What do we do now? The light has gone out of our lives," he paraphrases Nehru.

The mood in the bogie turns sombre and all the passengers sympathise with the mourning couple and their son. The obtrusive young man who had lost his temper on the woman looks on guiltily. The train has arrived at Guntakal and halts for a long time for a connecting train to arrive. The old woman looks at Alberto and holds his feet beseeching him to help her out with the formalities regarding her son's now dead body as they are strangers to the place and with no one to help them.

"You are the only one who displayed compassion towards us, in this mass of humanity. God will bless you," she pleads fervently with tears in her eyes. "Please help us."

We had under the circumstances, little choice but to help the needy souls. So with some degree of reluctance, we step out along with the three of them. We carry our luggage. They have nothing but pitiable looking bundles of cloth with them. Compared to them we look rich.

We soon learn that the Deccan Express and a local train bound for Hubli collided earlier in the the year,killing over fifty and injuring many more persons. The scene was a tangle of mangled metal.

We have a wash at the station followed by breakfast at the tea stall. As we got talking, the husband informs us that they had come here a few days earlier, but the police insisted on proof that they are the parents of the victim. They had to go back to their native place in Uttar Pradesh and come back with a certificate from the Village Sarpanch confirming their son's identity and that he was travelling on the train that met with the accident and providing other details. We learn, that it was the only body that had remained unidentified with no claimants.

We accompany the trio to the police station. It is around nine in the morning but Saheb has not yet arrived. So we wait patiently until around eleven when a short rotund man with a winglet moustache and well-ironed khaki uniform walks in. Everybody stands up and salutes him. We too stand up. After a considerable period of time, he calls us in. He recognises the trio without much ado and seeks the letter from the Sarpanch, which is handed over.

He reads it but does not seem to be fully satisfied. I think it may be a ruse to extort money. He goes inside holds a discussion with the other personnel and comes back to occupy his seat. He questions us about our relationship with the trio and we brief him about the events of the previous night. On seeing them and us, he must have realised that not much would be forthcoming as we had the looks of beggars about us.

He calls for the case papers relating to the accident and begins to question them.

"Now how old was your son?"

"Twenty three."

"Was he fat or thin, tall or short?"

"Thin, as tall as myself."

"Was he fair?"

"Not very."

"Does he have any marks on the body?"

"Yes."

"What type?"

"He has a long scar on the back of the left shoulder. He got it when a bull charged at him when he was about ten. He survived the bull only to be killed by the train," the father says through teary eyes. "Besides he has a black birth mark under the right armpit."

"Where was he going?"

"To Bangalore."

"Why?"

"To answer an interview."

"Where are his educational records?"

"He carried them with him. They may be in his bag in the wreckage. We tried to find it on our earlier visit when we came to see you but nothing was found as we had told you. We have brought his school leaving certificate in addition to the letter from our Sarpanch. Here it is" he says as he hands it over.

The inspector sends us to the morgue with two constables who were present at the questioning. He advises them to confirm the details given by the man, with the body. We also follow them. There are several bodies in various states of decomposition. The smell of death and decay is overpowering. The man without hesitation, points to one and says,

"That is him that's my Ajay."

His wife weeps uncontrollably, crying out loudly and repeatedly. "My son! My son! Why did you do this to us?"

The constables get the attendant to turn the body over. The body is naked and has a gaping wound below the neck. Two or three ribs poke out of the chest. Sure enough there is a scar on the left shoulder. The right arm is raised and a black birth mark reveals itself. The rest of the identification is a mere formality. We march back to the police station.

The constables report to the inspector. One of the constables draws a panchnama at the police station rather than at the morgue. The man signs it. It is clear the police are relieved to get rid of the body as an unidentified body means it has to remain, sometimes for years, and the capacity of the morgue is limited. Besides, the disposal of unidentified bodies is a tedious process and troublesome with no gain to the police.

We then return to the morgue where the body is handed over to the grieving family, against a receipt. The father takes out a clean white sheet from his bag and lays it on the floor. The body is placed on it. The sheet is folded to cover it. The mother breaks down hugging her son and weeping loudly. The father is not so loud but tears dripped from his eyes. The brother just looks on sad and lonely.

Having taken possession of the body, we assume we would be free to continue with our journey. But much to our dismay, the lady hangs on to Alberto's feet and pleads that we come to the crematorium as well. The police also send a constable with us. We hire a pickup, put the body in it and proceed to the crematorium which is in a dishevelled condition with firewood scattered in a disorderly manner. Fires of at least two earlier cremations are smoldering. The smell of burnt flesh suffuses the air. We pay for the pickup. The father performs the last rites and lights the fire. The mother is not allowed into the crematorium. The funeral home attendant tells us that the ashes could be collected only the next day as it was too late in the evening. Besides ashes take time to cool.

Back we march to the railway station. Sadly for us there is no train scheduled and we have to spend one more night on the platform. The family refuses to eat citing a religious taboo. We have a bath in the bathing facility at the station. The trunk is kept in the care of the family who group together at the far end of the platform. We have dinner and join the family stretching out on the platform. As we rest, the trio goes for a bath. It is difficult to get sleep with the constant and noisy movement of passenger and goods trains, more of the latter.

The next day, the family collects the ashes, ties it in a neat bundle and the mother hugs the ashes close to her body. The ashes are to be immersed in the river Ganga later, we are told. We bid the family farewell as they fall at our feet and weep thanking us through their tears. A train is due later in the day. We buy tickets and hang on at the rather poorly maintained and chaotic station.

It is afternoon as the train gathers speed. We are now in the heartland of the Deccan Plateau as the train cuts over a flat landscape. The terrain is bleak and bare after the crop has been harvested. The soil looks fertile but is begging for irrigation. We are two thousand feet above sea level. It is a hot evening as it is the peak of the summer season. The carriage shutters do not close properly and the cooling wind blows in freely providing a welcome respite from the heat

As the train makes several halts at wayside stations, people, mostly agricultural labourers and farmers move in and out. We find ourselves at Londa late afternoon. We alight along with our luggage. The train to Goa is several hours away, so we loiter around but cannot move too far carrying the luggage. The station is small and located in the midst of forests. The weather is cool, and less humid.

Alberto talks about his childhood, about his parents who are both dead he believes, and his only sibling a younger sister with whom he has lost touch due to the unfortunate sinking of the ship. He felt his parents must have died unaware that their son had survived the disaster. Communication was nonexistent in the war years.

On the other hand, I mention to him how the upbringing at Stanislaus was the best thing that could have happened to me. The Jesuits dealt with all students with a strong hand and enforced order and discipline. The country-wide reputation of the school was due to alumni who had shone in various fields and reached high positions. The school campus was large and at any time there were more than two thousand often unruly students. But on passing out, each one became an asset to society. For this reason, there was a huge demand for admissions to the school. For every student admitted at least two were rejected. The school was particularly known for its football and hockey teams. Many a player who had first hit the ball on its hallowed grounds had gone on to win laurels for the country.

As an orphan, I had to work for my upkeep and this made me an all-rounder as I learnt everything, including cooking, housekeeping, sports and music besides academics. Fr. O'Brien took me under his wing. He was my guardian angel.

Before I reached my SSCE, considering my interest in reading, I was put to work in the library. I appreciate the love of the Jesuits for detail and their thoroughness. The orphans are accommodated as per their aptitude so that upon leaving the orphanage they are prepared for the hard grind of life in the outside world. After SSCE I obtained a Diploma in Library Science. Fr. O'Brien takes me to the biggest bookshop in Bombay near Flora Fountain. As he walks in, the manager stands up and welcomes the priest. He is an aluminus of St. Stanislaus and knows Father O'Brien quite well, holding him in high esteem. He agrees to employ me initially as a temporary hand to be made permanent when a vacancy arises and subject to performance. And this enables me to pick up any book I like and read. The knowledge gained has kept me company.

"Your story of being an orphan dependent only on your paltry earnings from the bookshop somehow does not fit in. Is it not?" he queries.

I look at him failing to understand the point he is making. "Why do you say so?"

"Well did you not drop so much money for a poor beggar? Sometimes it was as much as rupees hundred a day but rarely less than fifty. It was a real bonanza, undreamt of. If you could contribute so much to a beggar how rich would you not be? Answer now," he commands.

It certainly is a sensible question. I had never thought of it. Clearly anyone in his position was entitled to ask it.

"Now, is not the time or place for it. But you will know it in due course."

He accepts my decision.

The train, delayed as usual, finally arrives and starts its journey in the early hours of the morning on a metre gauge track.

I miss seeing the Dudhsagar waterfalls which I was looking forward to, as we descend. The only sign of its presence is the roar of the waters as the train crosses a little bridge midway under the falls. Nothing is visible in the blackness of the night. We descend the ghats and finally arrive at Collem station where the steam engine needed to replenish its water supply, and has to halt for another train to pass. After considerable time, we get moving and reach Margao but darkness still prevails. The old man is all anxious. He keeps moving around the compartment. We have to disembark at the next railway station.

Chapter 3

At Majorda

The train is virtually empty as we halt. The name-board reads Majorda 13 mts. above MSL. Later I learn the acronym stands for Mean Sea Level. Darkness still envelopes the village. We descend on to the platform which too is empty except for a man huddled on a bench. The train puffs away on the last leg of its journey to end at Vasco da Gama terminus, a few stations away according to Alberto. We rest on another bench.

As the sky lightens, I can see a kutcha road running parallel to the railway station with a row of shops on the other side. There is movement in one of the shops. Smoke is coming out through a chimney rising above the roof. I can also get the sweet smell of baking bread through the smoke. I peep through the picket fence and a half open door confirms that it is a bakery. I am almost starving; I walk across the road and buy a few oven-hot loaves of bread. We hungrily devour a few. As the sun rises, a little teashop directly opposite to the entrance of the station also opens up. A fat fair man is sitting at the counter. Passengers start arriving at the station for the local train.

We have a wholesome breakfast at the teashop with a double serving of steaming pao-baji. We continue to sit for the arrival of the tea we have ordered. Alberto out of the blue says to no one in particular.

"Bless the Portuguese."

"But why?" I interpose

"I will tell you," he says. "The *pao baji* we ate would not exist if it was not for the Portuguese."

"Impossible. It is a typical Indian dish and so closely associated with the country throughout the world. How do the Portuguese come in?"

"Well, look, have you ever tasted a baji without potatoes chilies or tomatoes at or at least one of these? All these are products of plants native to South America which the Portuguese introduced to India. Now do you get me? And do you agree that the Indian curry would not exist without the chilly? And the Pao? Well it is Portuguese in name and make too."

I have to acknowledge his insight.

Hunger satisfied, now it was time to look for a place to stay. Back at the station a train has just left and the man huddling on the station bench is up and about. He looks curious with unkempt hair and beard and dressed in tatters. Being the only person present besides us, we approach him. He gives his name as Minguel Rod.

"That is not my real name but people call me so after a well known stage artiste, as I'm supposed to resemble him. To speak the truth, I have forgotten my own name," he says.

He is quite amiable. He appears to be the village vagrant and looks hungrily at us. I give him the remaining loaves. He gobbles them up.

There is a single storied tiled building across the road. A board hanging from the rafters of the first floor proclaims 'St Aloysius High School, Founded in 1924' written in white over a black background. The first floor railing is painted green. The ground floor has shops, all shut for the moment, one of which

hosts the Post Office. Another is a barber shop which has just opened for the day. We enter there and keep our luggage on the floor. The barber is an old man with a few front teeth missing. There are several petromax lanterns bearing the brand name Aida hanging from the roof along the wall in fact far too many even to work at night time which makes me question the barber who gives his name as Gopinath, whether the shop is open at night.

"Not at all," says he.

"Then why so many petromax?"

"Oh. I also provide lighting for *teatro** that take place quite frequently in this and neighbouring villages. That is actually the only entertainment for the villagers and an additional source of income to me," he concludes.

Alberto by all means needs a haircut and a shave. As he sits on the chair the barber inquires, "Polk or cut?"

"Well, polk."

The barber is not too happy with the state of the customer. But the seasoned barber gets on with his job. Alberto looks a different man within fifteen minutes. Hair trimmed beard shaved. And middle aged rather than old. Born again I tell him as he admires himself in the mirror. And unrecognizable from the beggar under the tree. And definitely presentable. And so much the better if we have to secure a place to stay in the village.

"How do you like it now?"

"Very well. Thank you."

We pay him and walk out.

We find a comfortable place to rest at the end of the platform where Alberto opens the trunk, checks everything. The cloth bags containing the coins are very much there but he seems to be a bit doubtful and opens one. And then the other. He gives out a cry and gapes open-mouthed at me. Instead of the coins, the bags now contain stones, the type used as ballast on the

---

* Konkani Drama

railway tracks. Neither of us can comprehend the meaning but both understand the implication and its impact on our lives.

Minguel sees that we are disturbed and comes close. But we cannot tell him our situation. He assures us on being asked that there are quite a few *Bhatkars* who have outhouses which could be leased. He promises to take us to the best among them. He tells us that he acts as a coolie at the station and offers to carry our luggage. We cannot refuse such a good offer being tired and in shock.

We cross the tracks. There is no road whatsoever. All we can see is a beaten footpath in between coconut trees with small pathways branching off in different directions. The village seems to be in slumber. To be honest there is barely a village. A thatched hut is the first habitation we pass by. Further, there is a larger house with a little board indicating *Taverna Licenciada* after which there is a single storied modern house. A tall fair bearded man polishig a gun in the porch, drew my attention as he looked so much like Fidel Castro. Two pretty little girls were playing besides him. We walk may be three quarters of a mile through virtual emptiness passing seven to eight little houses in all with the surroundings clean and neat.

We continue to follow him but find it difficult to keep pace as he takes quick strides despite his advancing age and the load on his head. We finally arrive at a large rambling house, which seems to have seen better days. The house has a balcao with a cement floor which can be reached over a flight of stairs. A compound wall encloses the house with a jackfruit tree on one side runeala plum trees on the other. A pomelo tree can be seen towards the corner full with football shaped fruit. Crotons and decorative plants abound. He keeps our luggage down and calls out to the *bhatkar**.

After a short time, a tall man who must be in his early fifties answers the call and greets us. He occupies the easy chair in

---

* Landlord

the balcao. He is fairly dark complexioned, square jawed with a receding hairline. He beckons to us. We climb the stairs. We shake hands. He inquires whether we will have tea or coffee.

"Tea," shouts out Minguel before we can open our mouths.

"We have just had breakfast at the teashop opposite the railway station," replies Alberto.

"Does not matter. Another cup will do no harm. Minguel Rod will need company," says the *Bhatkar* and calls out to the housemaid.

"With or without milk?" asks the maid.

"Without," says Minguel.

"So be it," says Alberto.

Minguel then explains that we have come looking for a room to stay.

The questions begin slow and steady

"Where do you come from?"

"Bombay."

"Are there more or just the two of you?"

"Just us."

"Are you Goans?"

"Well, yes," after a bit of hesitation as my pedigree is in question.

"Why have you come to Goa?"

"Because I have my house and land here," butts in Alberto

"Where?"

"That is the problem. I used to come here when my parents were alive. Now I am coming after a quarter of a century. I plan to locate it."

"How do you know you are from Majorda?"

"My father was a member of Club Boa Morte at Jer Mahal building Dhobitalao in Bombay. And I too am member of the club. People from outside the village are not eligible for membership. Besides I remember my village clearly."

"Your father's name?"

"Basil da Costa."

"I do not recollect any person by the name."

"He was rarely in Goa."

"How long will you stay"

"I do not know."

"What do you mean?"

"As I have said our house is in this village. We have to trace it, check its condition and if it is habitable, move in."

"How much rent will you pay"

"As you are the owner, it is for you to fix the rent."

"How much can you afford."

"Rupees seven per month."

"Very low, but let it be."

Satisfied the *Bhatkar* calls the maid and asks, "Which of the rooms are empty?"

"If it is for someone to live in, then the one in the corner will be better. It is in good shape but may need doing up here and there."

"Take these persons and show them the room. If it suits them clean it up. Go follow her. The room has not been occupied for long and may not be immediately habitable. Give them whatever help is needed," are his parting words

He requests us to take a look and confirm if that will do. We walk through the compound to the rear of the house where there are rows of rooms built at the end of the wall. They seem to serve as store rooms for coconuts. We are directed to the last one. The maid of the house opens the door, we peep in. It is dark. The village is not electrified.

The room is large made of mud walls and a roof of country tiles. The wall facing the south has a window. The floor needs to be made up and there are cobwebs and accumulated dust covers the floor. Evidently, the room has not been occupied for long. Considering our situation we accept the offer and immediately begin making the room slightly more habitable. The room looks neat and clean within an hour. The maid offers to do up the floor with a layer of cow dung and in the meantime we are offered the verandah of the house to sleep for the night.

We keep our luggage in the room (nothing valuable inside now) and walk back to the railway station with Minguel Rod. We pay him double of what he asks for. The bazaar is just behind the railway station with a few shops. He takes us to the shop of a man called Kantu on the ground floor of the school building a jovial looking old man in a dhoti. We buy candles, rice, chillies, tea powder and sugar from his rather large shop. We proceed to another shop some distance away to buy pots and other essentials. From another shop we purchase mats as we make our way back to our new abode. The maid has in the meantime applied a coat of cow dung to the floor of the room and kept the door and window open for quick drying.

The impact of the transformation of coins into stones hits us harder as we go to sleep in the verandah. We wake up still in a disconcerted frame of mind as the sun rises to a raucous call of cuckoos soon joined by magpie robins and tree-pies. Thankfully we had examined the trunk at the railway station itself. Otherwise the maid and even the *Bhatkar* would be suspects in our minds.

The house itself is evidently old with no toilet attached. Instead, the toilets located on the perimeter of the compound have pigs attached. I can see how pretty the countryside is. Coconut trees everywhere as far as the eye can see. Some banyan, jackfruit and mango trees appear to be interlopers. The backyard is all fowl play, chicken, ducks and a couple of turkeys. A sow with her piglings is wallowing in the muck resulting from the waste water discharged from the house. A cow is tethered in the cowshed at the corner of the compound. The calf frolics around nudging the banana plants with its head from time to time.

Before long the *Bhatkar* appears as we are about to settle in our room. He suggests that we make an extension of thatch to one side of the room to serve as a kitchen since cooking inside the room may make the room too smoky. He points out beyond the compound to a bamboo grove from which we may cut bamboos for the purpose and use the dry coconut leaves stacked nearby, for thatch.

"But be careful," he warns. "There are fowls and turkeys, swine and canine freely moving around and they may finish your lunch before you do."

As he turns back, he calls us to follow him. He takes us by the side of his house to another room, gives us a table, four chairs and a kerosene lamp with a chimney. As we are about to carry the furniture away a lady thrusts her head out through the window and calls out to him.

"Why don't you also give them a sofa and some Macau crockery too?"

The *Bhatkar* winks at us and tells us to move on with the furniture. On the way back, Alberto points out that the behaviour of the wife is a natural consequence of her husband being gullible and overly trusting and helpful even to people he does not know, like us.

We are soon busy erecting the extension against the wall on the western side. I borrow the machete from the *Bhatkar*, and cut half a dozen bamboos and trim them. Alberto in the meantime excavates the foundations. We fix the bamboo poles in. But we need twine to secure the poles and the thatch.

I have to rush to the bazaar. I borrow *Bhatkar*'s bicycle. Halfway there, I realise I would be better off on foot as the cycle is difficult to ride through the sand. But I have no choice. I pedal on. I buy jute twine and hurry back. Soon the skeleton is ready entirely of bamboo secured with twine. We bring coconut leaves from the stack in the *Bhatkar*'s property and cover the roof. We strap coconut leaves to the sides and enclose the extension. We are ready.

Two days of sleeping in the verandah and now time to shift into the room as the cow dung applied to the floor has dried up and the extension is erected. The room now looks comfortable with a table and chairs. But I can smell decaying flesh with every gust of wind. May be some dead animal is putrefying in the vicinity, I think.

Alberto sits on one of the chairs and looks out through the window with a lost look. I can understand how he must be feeling after the loss of the money. Suddenly, he jumps picks up the trunk lifts it and places it on the table. He then empties it of its contents. There is a thick brown paper stuck to the bottom of the trunk which he tears open. His eyes glow as he picks up two envelopes with currency notes in it. His joy is visible on his face.

"Look." he says. "I had exchanged some of the coins earlier into notes and then hidden here, just in case. And I forgot about it altogether until this moment. We now at least have sufficient money to tide over our immediate needs."

At this point I explain to him how I could afford to put so much money into his bowl despite my meagre salary, an answer I had earlier deferred. He refuses to believe me.

'How can that ever be?"

"Do you believe that you can see now while you could not see for the previous twenty-five years?"

"Yes very much."

"Did any doctor cure you?"

"No."

"So your cure cannot be explained. Likewise, with bottlecaps turning into coins. The same principle has worked whether you believe it or not."

"Well I have to acknowledge it. And I believe you. And this explains another mystery. Now I understand why I found the internal cork packing of bottle caps with contributions you made."

Chapter 4

Football Match

From the window, I can see that some boys have gathered outside kicking a ball. I jump over the window, and over the compound wall, like I'm still in school. Soon, I reach the rudimentary playground where two bamboo poles on either side with a string tied on top serve as goal-posts. The half dozen coconut trees placed on the ground act as dummy players. Regular play has raked up the sand.

After some time there is a break in the game and the boys more or less of my age, come around and look at me inquisitively. Fortunately, many of my boarding mates in Bombay were Goans from whom I picked up Konkani and can speak the language as fluently as any Goan And I can swear perhaps even better then these local boys! When the boys learn that I have come from Bombay they are impressed and their curiosity is aroused even more.

"Do you play cricket?" asks one rather dark boy.

"Of course, I do."

"And hockey?"

"Why not? Indeed my school dominates hockey in Bombay."

"And you do not play football?"

"A little. I am not particularly good. Can I play with you all?"

"Yes, come on join us."

Most of the boys are pretty good with the ball and are natural talents but one can see they have had no benefit of coaching. Roque is short and wiry. A great dribbler. Antonio has a powerful kick with the left foot. Caetano and Minguel are passable. José is erratic but energetic. Domingo in goal is a bit slow and rarely rushes out to foil an attack. Vincent is speedy with great ball sense. At the other end, a girl, Severina, stands in the goal. There is a shortage of players. They soon realise that I am a better player than all of them and that makes them even happier, because they have a game coming up against the boys from a neighbouring ward later in the month. So I also take up as coach.

It is nearing the end of the month and it is time for the football game. We have been practicing these last few days under my guidance. The team from the other ward is supposedly strong and has beaten our team for the last five times succesively over a period of one year. The match scheduled for half past four only starts at quarter past five on our ground. The players of the other team are older than our boys and seem to be quite adept at the game.

Although I can play in any position, I prefer to marshall the defence with José to my left and Manuel on the right. Roque and Caetano play as halves, while Antonio and Lourenco are the forwards. Domingo ideally built is, the goal keeper. The ground is much smaller than normal, hence only eight players.

I am the only unknown quantity as all the players know each other as also each other's game. The match starts at a furious pace and we are able to withstand the onslaught in the

first half which ends scoreless. Our side is happy with the play but our opponents had expected to take a big lead as can be seen from their supporters' gloom.

The second half begins and I choose to move up to the forward line while Manuel comes in the defence. We concede a goal in the third minute after resumption to the joy of the opposition supporters. Time for me to prove my mettle as a footballer with the Bombay junior team.

Within the next seven minutes we restore parity and are one up with a goal each scored by Roque with his head and Antonio with a lethal left foot kick, both from my passes. The opponents cannot believe what has hit them and are all charged up as they leave their defence open and move forward to seek an equaliser. I take advantage of the situation, pick up a loose ball near the half line, use my superior speed to outrun the defenders giving chase, and score.

The final score is three to one in our favour. I am the toast of the local supporters. The opponents are disheartened to suffer an unexpected defeat.

As days go by, I become part of the local boys group who seem to be in awe of my Bombay upbringing and my fluency in English. We become good friends and they are quite happy to listen to my stories about the great city Bombay to which none of them have been, but they have heard so much about city.

I do feel that I should secure some employment at least to keep myself busy. And I mention this to *Bhatkar* when I meet him later.

"Any job will do," I tell him.

He asks me to be present the next morning when the baker comes.

Before the sun rises, I am outside the *Bhatkar's* house, as soon as I hear the cling-cling as the baker hammers his staff on the ground. The *Bhatkar's* wife collects her loaves and heads back inside. The *Bhatkar* requests the baker, who is not the same one who has a bakery near the station, to find some employment for me. This one is from Betalbatim. He offers to take me as an apprentice sales boy as one of his regular salesmen has secured a driver's job in Kuwait.

The next day, I am at the baker's by five in the morning. I have to accompany him from house to house so that I may learn the route. This happens for two days. On the third day, I am on my own. As I deliver the loaves to each of the houses, I calculate my earnings which are ten paisa for every rupee worth of loaves sold. It was a good incentive. But I had the most painful experience when I reach a particular not too impressive house.

The landlady orders a dozen loaves which I neatly provide her. She counts them and asks me to recount. I count up to twelve. She looks at me and questions, "Is that a dozen?"

"Of course it is," I say.

At this she twists my ears like they have never been twisted before, even by the worst of teachers in my school. It hurts real bad. She then calls her husband and pointing to me says:

"Look what education does to this class. I ask for a dozen

loaves and this imp gives me only twelve. And on top reaffirms that he is right. Look at the impertinence. "And you", pointing her forefinger at her husband, "are for educating the masses. Is it not?"

I turn back, stop delivering more loaves and return the bread basket to the baker. I no more want to be a bread man. My apprenticeship is ended.

Back in the room, I explain the happenings to Alberto, who bursts out laughing.

"Did you not know that a baker's dozen is thirteen and not twelve?"

And to think that I always thought thirteen was the devil's dozen!

"Perhaps that particular lady is the devil incarnate I mumble to myself. Is that the reason why Goans are called *maca pao* in Bombay?" I ask in anger.

Chapter 5

The Village and the Pigs

One day as I stroll around after breakfast. I see the *Bhatkar* watering the garden. I walk towards him. He is affable and loves to talk.

"Do you like to read?" he asks.

"Most certainly I do," is my response. "I worked as a librarian."

"Come on in, I will show you my library."

As I walk in with him, the wife looks at me dubiously. "How many times have I not told you not to bring anyone inside the house?" she calls out in anger.

She is ignored as we walk in. The library is a long room lined with well stocked book shelves. The books are dog eared and placed in a disorderly way, an indicator that the books are actually read. But he seems to find whatever he wants at a glance. "My library needs to be put in order," says he. I offer to do it for him. He gladly accepts.

I am busy the next few days identifying the books by their subjects aligning them properly and cataloguing them. *Bhatkar* is extremely happy with my work. He permits me to take away any book to read and return. He pays me generously for my efforts. Over the next few weeks as I interact with the *Bhatkar* I realise he is not merely a landlord but rather an institution. His balcao is always flooded with people with problems. And he listens patiently and tries to find solutions. It is virtually a courtroom.

It is his wife who looks after the home affairs and the family while her husband serves the world around him, much to her dismay.

As I leave, the stink of rotting flesh again floats in with the breeze. It is much stronger now and I almost puke. As it continues to persist, I draw the attention of *Bhatkar* to it, since he does not seem to notice it.

"Nothing much to be worried about," he says. "Such stink is common here this time of the year. It will disappear after a few weeks," he adds.

"You know this village is reputed for the quality of its watermelons and this stink is the price that has to be paid to attain the quality."

I do not understand how sweet watermelons may be related to such offensive smell. And I say so.

Bhatkar provides the answer. "The villagers put offal and other waste meat into gunny bags and drop the bags into the water holes dug to provide water to the vines that produce the watermelons. The meat rots and emits the stink that pervades the air."

"The rotting waters provide fertilizer for the watermelon vines and flood the village with the stink. And that is how the top quality watermelons are produced. The water holes are filled up before the monsoons. The following years new water holes are dug at a different location."

I am intrigued and ask "where could I get more information about the village?"

"Why not here in the library itself? Why don't you sit down? Let me tell you." And he begins an interesting narration.

"The lovely village called Calata, together with Majorda forms a Parish, Mae de Deus and with Utorda, the three constitute a single Panchayat.

"The etymology of the village names becomes apparent, if one looks at the original Konkani names – *Khala'ta, Mazo'dde, Utor'dde* which means, the lower part, middle part and the northern part. That is the layout of the village, as it slumbers along the Arabian Sea."

He goes on.

"The village is ancient and figures in the Ramayana. Like the Bible, the Ramayan has several versions. One such version each is preserved in its original form, under Codices Nos.771 and 772 in the District Archives of Braga in Northern Portugal."

He requests me to bring the book, Konkani Literature in Roman Script by Prof. Olivinho Gomes from the book shelf

I give it to him.

He shuffles through the pages until he comes to what he is looking for. Quoting from the text he narrates:

It gives great prominence to Lav and Kush, the sons of Rama and Sita, and the latter consigned to the forests along with them, and their brave fight against their oppressor father's armies. It brings Sri Rama as a child into Goan territory, as abducted by diabolic daityas and makes him to meet with the Goan gaunkars of Utorda and Majorda villages, when the son of Ravana, Indrojit, makes an attempt to kidnap the young Rama to Sri Lanka through Mormugao, until rescued by Sri Vashistha, his preceptor, and taken back home to his native Ayodhya.

He returns the book and I keep it back in its proper place in the shelf. He resumes:

"The village saw a revolutionary change in its ancient and

archaic living pattern, when the missionaries from the Society Of Jesus arrived, towards the last quarter of the sixteenth century.

"The Jesuits were a diligent and studious breed. Before entering a village they made a deep study of its caste composition, habits, customs and practices. And their approach was modeled to suit the temperament of the village. The presiding deity of the village was *Maha-mai* (Mother Goddess) so the villagers were offered Mother of God in her place as the patroness.

"By 1588 the entire village had freely embraced Christianity, without any resistance. The old temple dedicated to *Mahamai* (Mother Goddess) was demolished as it served no further purpuse and a church dedicated to *Mae de Deus* (Mother of God) was built, in its place by the villagers on the architectural plans prepared by the missionaries. The missionaries had shrewdly surmised that the villagers would find it easier to transfer their allegiance from Mother Goddess to Mother of God. And that is what happened."

"A relic of the Pre-Portuguese past is preserved in the museum at Old Goa in the form of a sati stone from the village."

Bhatkar then talks at length about other villages. But the same has no bearing on this narration except in so far as it relates to Betalbatim.

Bhatkar tells me, "The village to the South was dedicated to Betal a pre Hindu diety of the indigenous people. Hence the name of the village *Betalbhat* (land of *Betal*) which the Portuguese spelt as Betalbatim. The church is dedicated to Our Lady of Remedios. But it has a side altar dedicated to St Bartolomeu the apostle of Christ. And the feast is celebrated in a grand manner on the last Sunday of August. If you ask anyone in the village you will be told, it is the feast of *São Betal*. St Bartolomeu has been appropriated and projected as *São Betal*. It was easier for the new converts to accept their previous diety transformed into a Catholic saint!"

He then picks up another book 'India and the West: The First Encounters' by Joséph Velimkar, opens a page and gives the book to me. I read:

Some churches drew crowds and soon became famous as pilgrimage centres. The earliest to gain this distinction was the Mother of God chapel at Majorda. In 1593 it was described as follows:

'...Christians of the region having a singular devotion to her (Mary) and because this church is in the middle of Salcete the crowds, who flocked to this spacious church specially on Saturdays, could not even be accommodated inside its four walls. If sometimes more priests happen to go to celebrate Mass there, the church gets full again and again. Some people come in very reverently. On entering the parvis they kneel immediately, bend to the ground and walk on their knees to the church door. After Mass the priest recites the litany of Our Lady and preaches a sermon. The people remain very attentive." (ARSI Goa 14.f.78r-78v)

The Bhatkar resumes the narrative, "Oral tradition goes that Italian Missionaries had set up a bakery in Majorda and given training to members of the Vaishya community who were sweetmeat makers.

These people found the task easy, as making sweetmeats, also required the kneading of dough. And then, these well trained persons spread to every nook and corner of the territory. To make bread. And to bake bread. And, thus my village came to be the bread basket of Goa."

He goes on, "Son, if ever you are lost in Goa, just put your nose up in the air, smell the sweet flavour of baking bread and follow it. Knock on the door, and a Mazoddekar* will open it for you."

"That was my father's advice as a young boy. As I grew up and moved all over Goa, I realised my father was right." Bring me Ethnogaphy of Goa by A B Braganza Pereira," he urges.

---

* a native of Majorda

I recall the title as I had glanced over it and was keen to read it. I find it easily in the third shelf of the first bookcase.

"Go through it. Take the book, but see that you return it. It is very informative and well sourced," he advises.

"He was an eminent jurist and ethnographer who has his ancestral roots in Utorda village. He confirms in this epochal book that the Catholics of Kshatriya and Vaishya descent together constitute the Chardo caste. And these are the gaonkars of the village. The gaonkars are the original settlers who cleared the jungles and made the land habitable and cultivable. Being the first arrivals they cornered all the land. The surplus land was kept in common ownership and was leased to later arrivals."

"Like others, our village too is agrarian. But what makes us a class apart is the quality of our watermelons. Have you ever traveled along the main road from Margao to Panjim? You will find scores of villagers with heaps of watermelons by the road side inviting you to buy them.

Stop for a moment. The vendor will invariably entice you with the appetiser, 'it is from Utorda'. For generations, Utorda has been to watermelons what Kashmir or Simla is to apples. Later, a person from the village running a bakery in Parra is believed to have introduced the practice, in that village. And thus, Parra has become the Utorda of North Goa".

"The other contribution of the village is in the field of western music. The musical instruction begins at the parochial school. Many a young musical talent has migrated to Bombay and moved over to film music. Whenever you relax at a movie you could be practically certain that our villager has some role in the music which is keeping you entertained.

And before I finish let me tell you that the Portuguese came to Goa upon invitation extended to them by Mhal Pai and Timoja Nayak local leaders. Later the family of Timoja settled at the extreme northen end of Calata. Their descendants continue to live in their ancestral house."

I am glad that I got a full resume of the whole village in just one sitting with one man.

After the departure of Fr. O'Brien I have preferred to be alone 'all all alone' when the occasion permitted walking the hills or whatever was left of them in Bandra. But in Goa the countryside invites and offers you solitude aplenty. I put on my beret for the dew and my binoculars for the view as I step out into the cool air. I often wish this February weather lasts all year round.

The pathway is narrow, sand deep and the prickly thistles form a mock avenue. The Stereculia stands tall with a perfect canopy of drooping branches, shorn of leaf. Kidney shaped pods, red and ripe, hang on the branches. Some open up and gently let the cylindrical seeds, dressed in grey jacket and brown underwear, drop to earth a good fifty feet below. A single serpent eagle perched on a drooping branch seems to wait for the sun to rise higher. The coppersmith barbet can be heard, not seen, as usual.

The coconut grove descends into the paddy fields, dry and bare. The fields have been harvested and are full of paddy stubble. The pond on the margin is drying up. A marsh sand piper is alert to my approach before I have seen it, and flies away with a song.

The silk cotton tree has laid a pink buffet for its avian guests. It always does so in February. And I have always spent time in the vicinity of the few trees found on Bandra hill. But in Goa I can see specks of pink everywhere. Dozens of avian denizens have arrived for a gourmet breakfast. The pesky crows are raucous as ever. The starlings arrive by and by. The golden oriole is conspicuous by its colour. I await the arrival of other invitees.

Behind me,the façade of the Nossa Senhora dos Remedios Church rises. The rays of the rising sun make their first appearance through the fog. I count over a hundred birds, and a dozen species on a single tree. My trip is done.

On my way back I notice that every house has a pigsty. The pigs not only clean up the toilets but are also a source of meat and money to the families.

Every house has a fish plate hanging from a rafter at the rear of the house. The fish plates are easy to find strewn along the railway tracks. When struck by a bolt, which otherwise is used to fasten the rails, it gives a ringing sound. Every time the bell is rung, pigs come running in to be fed. I watch pigs foraging in the fields and coconut groves and plowing the soil with their snouts in large groups, but each pig seems to have an uncanny ability to identify its own ring of the bell. The bells keep ringing at different houses at different times. It is only the pigs attached to that house that run while the others continue to forage unconcerned.

The bells make similar ringing tones and for a human it is difficult to differentiate between the tones. I have even tried ringing the bells myself from different households and it is only the pigs attached to that house that come rushing in. How do the pigs do it? I still do not have an answer. Perhaps George Orwell understood the pigs better.

T*h*e Sc*h*ool

After my first job as a baker ended in a total fiasco *Bhatkar* tells me that the local school is looking for a librarian to set its library in order.

"Would you be able to help?" he requests.

"Would be glad to," I reply.

"Go and meet the principal of the school whenever convenient. Tell him that I have recommended you."

On Monday morning I find myself below the staircase that leads up to the school. Two flights of stairs and I am up there. The school peon has opened the gate and the classrooms. He tells me the principal will arrive a little later. The wooden floor of the school is strong, but a few planks are a little loose. I stand in the verandah and watch students arrive.

Standing on the first floor I have a great view of the railway station not more than fifteen yards away, just across the road. The train arrives noisily, belching thick black smoke and steam. I look on, enraptured by the fact that water with the mere application of heat can generate so much of power to push such a heavy train over long distances. More people get in, than get out of the train. And those that get out are mostly students, who hurry across the road and up the stairs. The train is on time. Over the next few days I realise that when the train is late the classrooms are half empty when classes begin.

A fish-plate hangs in one corner. The peon strikes it with the big bolt. Students, (and not pigs!) rush in. Classes begin. As the principal has not come, I descend the stairs. I need a haircut. Gopinath is reading *Gomantak* a Marathi newspaper. I am the first customer for the day. This is only my second visit to his saloon but the first haircut. He does not recognize me. When I tell him I have come to meet the principal he gets talking.

"It is a great school. My son Shekhar studies there. The students are reputed to be the most disciplined. The principal sees to that. He is very strict. Parents of unruly children bring their children here. And in no time they fall in line. There, there, he comes." He points to a not too tall man with sparse hair who comes riding a red Jawa motorcycle.

After I am done with Gopinath I ascend the staircase to the school. The principal is in his office-a little cubicle by the side of the staircase. I am called in and asked the purpose of my visit. A name plate Vishnudas S Kunkoliemkar-Principal, stands atop his simple desk. He is glad I have come. I am shown the library which is in quite a disorder and needs streamlining. I offer to do it. I tell him that I will do it as an honorary task. He has been to Bombay several times but not seen my former school. He has heard of it as one of the premier educational institutions in that city.

I have a very busy few days. Teachers too help me during their off period. I meet the teachers at interval in the staff room. Tall, fair and strictly formal and stern Fatima teaches French. Equally fair with a reddish facial tone and slightly shorter and wearing a shorter dress is science teacher Ninette who tells me she has recently joined. She has a perennial smile on her

face and students seem to be overtly fond of her. V V Lotlikar is the second science teacher-balding and jovial. Students call him Boyer after a famous Goan actor M Boyer who himself took the stage name from an English actor Charles Boyer. Anil Pai a Hindi teacher too is a recent recruit full of youthful energy. Teacher Lima is among the more senior teachers.

And there is George Anthony Moses rather dark for an Anglo-Indian, the grand-dad of the school. A good natured fellow who is fond of asking anyone in a hurry, "Young man why are you in a hurry? If you could wait for nine months why can't you wait for a few minutes?"

I learn that the school was initially run in Betalbatim. It was shifted to Majorda soon after the second liberation of Goa in 1961. As such, the school does not have the type of campus we associate with schools in Bombay. But in spite of this short-coming the school is reputed as being among the best in rural Goa. Besides Majorda and Utorda ,students from distant places like Vasco, Dabolim, Cansaulim, Velcao, Bogmalo, apart from the neighbouring villages attend the school. The principal turns out not only to be a disciplinarian but also generous as he puts an envelope in my front pocket despite my protestations.

"I like your work Can you work for the school as a part-time librarian thrice a week? We cannot offer much," he adds.

"I shall be glad to," is my quick response.

"You can work on Monday, Wednesdays and Fridays or would you like a different schedule?"

I am happy with the schedule.

Chapter 7

The Tailor And The Choir Master

Our first few weeks in Goa have gone and it is certainly for the first time that I have not attended Sunday church service for so long. I feel guilty. And I broach the subject with Alberto. The difficulty is that he does not have any worthwhile clothes to wear to church. The next morning we take the first train to Margao. We walk along a concrete road with little decrepit shops lining it on either side. We have breakfast at Bombay Café and as we do so, Alberto talks of M. D'Costa cloth shop with which he was not unfamiliar in his younger days.

Breakfast over, we proceed a short distance away to the Municipal market. As the shops are still closed we bide our time at *Pimplla-pedd* where Hindus converge for worship. By 10 o'clock the shops are open and as we enter the market, the M. D'Costa's shop is to our right. Alberto buys two trouser length pieces, grey and dark blue, and two shirt pieces, white and light blue for himself, and a grey trouser piece and a white shirt piece for me. We also buy some towels. Alberto remembers a tailoring shop owned by his school friend. As we walk, the first imposing edifice in town comes into view. It is the Municipal building points out Alberto. The tailor's shop is by its side with a board proclaiming *Alfaiataria Costa*. It is a lone tailor working who takes our measurements and says he will take about three weeks to deliver the trousers and shirts.

Alberto pleads for an earlier date but is rebuffed as the tailor says he has pendng orders to fulfill. And, he is short of helpers at the shop.

"Where do you get tailors anymore? The moment a young man has learnt to thread a needle, he goes to Kuwait or some place abroad. Earlier it was East Africa. And poses as a master tailor! Among the blind, one who can merely thread a needle poses as a fashion designer. It is big money there. No one wants to work here in Goa. The days when a father would walk in with his son in tow to work as a tailor are over," he complains bitterly.

At this time Alberto calls the tailor by his first name Sebastiao and asks him, "Do you not remember me?"

The tailor is in difficulty. "Did you not study at *Escola Primaria* at Calata?"

"Yes I did," says Sebastiao.

"And do you not remember Alberto and the fight you had with him?"

"I do," says Sebastiao.

"I am Alberto!"

"But Alberto died during the war when his ship was sunk."

"Have you not taken my measurements and confirmed that I am alive? I was dead for the world but am alive for myself." says Alberto.

The tailor looks on dubiously.

"How can I be sure you are not an impostor? Such a thing happened in Verna not long ago. A man came and claimed to be the husband of a lady whose husband had disappeared decades earlier. He did look like her husband though. He convinced her that he was her husband by telling her some past stories which he apparently had learnt from her school mate who was working with him in Calcutta. The woman was convinced and began to live with him.

"He was exposed when her school mate returned to Goa and visited her. And there was hell to pay. He was arrested. And it came out that he had duped another lady too and decamped with her gold."

"Alright," says Alberto, "You ask me questions about our school life."

"Who were our teachers?"

"João Cota from Betalbatim and Dona Alzira from Calata"

"Name the female both of us were interested in and which was the cause of the fight between us."

"Anna."

"Name at least three classmates."

"Cruz from Guirim, Pascoal from Calata and Serafina from Curilo."

"Well, you must be him. This must be only the second case of resurrection. And I suppose that makes me a doubting Thomas."

Both of them hug each other, sit down and talk animatedly about their school days and about how life has changed over the years. Sebastiao promises to deliver at least a trouser and a shirt each in two days time.

Before leaving Alberto inquires. 'Tell me what happened to Anna? Did you marry her?"

"Oh, no!"

'Who did she marry?'

'Son of a rich tailor who had returned from Kenya. Now they are in Toronto Canada.'

"Does she come down?"

"I did meet her once. But she failed to recognize me until I reminded her. But you she remembered and inquired about. She appeared to be well off. She could not speak Konkani either."

'Oh that does happen when a poor girl marries a rich boy!"

'There is an apt song on this theme by Peter Sarstedt recently released *Where Do You Go to (My Lovely)?*" I tell Alberto.

Two days later we are back at the tailor's shop. The tailor is surprised to see us so early.

"Nothing is ready. Come by six," says he.

So we have a full day to explore Margao. To me it appears to be a glorified village. There is not a single concrete building except for the Gomant Vidya Niketan and the Comunidade buildings. The rest are all tiled structures designed like chawls for commercial shops. There are just two or three single-storied buildings along the road to the railway level crossing. Another houses a Cinema theatre called Cine Lata on the upper floor with shops on the ground floor.

We then enter the general market with little shops selling local produce and groceries. There is a row of bakers on one side and a little corner selling sausages. Footwear and cloth shops too exist. We have lunch at a restaurant called Venice, a quiet and homey place with a fair, thick lipped, curly haired, lady at the counter. The fish-curry-rice is tasty.

We still have a few hours to endure. And the municipal garden comes in handy. It is split into two by a passage in between. The southern part facing the municipal building is called Praca Jorge Barreto and the northern part, the Aga Khan Park, so named in honour of The Aga Khan who had visited Goa. The local Ismaili community had acquired the land and gifted it to the municipality to commemorate the visit of their religious head as stated on a commenorative plaque. It is not six yet, so there is time for a cup of tea. From the passage we proceed towards Grace Church which has shops on its periphery. We stare at *Marliz* the celebrated Coffee Shop. We walk in and order a cup of coffee each with slices of cake. I have never tasted such coffee even in the great city of Bombay. Marvelous.

We collect our clothes – perfect fit for both of us. He declines to accept payment.

"I cannot accept payment from a ghost!" he says good

humouredly.

"And you are the only tailor who stitches clothes for a ghost!" responds Alberto. Both hug each other as we leave.

We travel home late in the evening by the last train.

The following Sunday, we walk to the Church of Mae de Deus, a little distance from the railway station in our new clothes. It is a pretty big structure with a white-washed facade but full with very little space even for standing. The villagers are seemingly devout. Both of us are more interested in the choir and their singing, than the Mass. We inch our way towards the altar to be able to see and listen to the choir. There is no sound system, unlike in Bombay. The choir master is elderly but the choir is pretty good. Alberto realises that there is no scope for him to step in as choir master as the church is well served.

The next Sunday, we cross the paddy fields that lie just about a hundred yards away from our residence, to reach the Church of the neighbouring village.The white façade of the Church overlooks the paddy fields. We are sufficiently in time to get the front seats and have a better look at the choir. There is no choir master and the group of motley singers has neither direction nor harmony in their singing.

After the last mass is over, we meet the *Padre Vigario*. Alberto explains to him that he was a musician on the ship and now lives in Calata, just across the paddy fields. He offers to be the choir master. The *Padre Vigario* seems to feel that his prayers have been answered and offers the job on a salary of fifty rupees per month for a trial period of three months to be later increased. The choir master has to train the choir and be present for all Sunday masses. Wedding and funeral services will have to be attended if required and will be paid separately.

Besides, the choir master has to teach in the parochial music school where he will be paid his fees separately through a collection from the students. There was no way to refuse.

The choir master only requests the *Padre Vigario* to allow me to assist and if need be to teach in his absence.

The *Padre Vigario* looks at me and questions as to how at my age, I could be teaching music. I tell him that I studied music at St. Stanislaus at Bombay under Fr. O'Brien and that I could give a demonstration in the weeks ahead. He is highly impressed when I name my school.

Chapter 8

On the beach

It's late May, the heat and the humidity are rising day by day. The weather is unbearable as the monsoon too is delayed. I am perspiring as if I am the Dudhsagar falls. The boys suggest a romp on the beach as it would be cooler. So we march on along a broad pathway choreographed in white sand that slaloms around coconut trees, slithers under stalactites of banian tree roots hanging from fanned out branches, tunnels through an overgrowth of under bush and opens on to the beach. My feet sink deep up to the ankles in the sand and the walk becomes tiring. I am accustomed to walking on the hard pavements of Bombay. But my friends seem to be quite comfortable.

The sea is separated from the landmass by nature's own fortification a green wall of pandanus cycads, survivors from the Jurassic era forming the first line of defence, in the unceasing war between land and sea. But as we approach the shore the cycads appear more like a forest than a fortification.

Hiding under the thick foliage in the leaf litter below the cycads are nocturnal creatures like the jackals. There is a solitary black-caped night heron dozing with its neck retracted between its wings on an outstretched branch of the casuarina above the stream, which drains the waters of the village into the sea. The sand dunes emerge huge and conical like the breasts of sleeping giantesses covered in green brassieres of goat's feet creepers with floral designs in pink, which seem to heave as the wind rustles through them. The dunes piled up in the manner of battle tanks under green camouflage form the second line of defence against the marauding waves.

Fishing nets are drying on the beach. Fishermen are scattered in every direction doing various chores. Some are greasing the boats with a strong-smelling oily liquid which I learn is the extract of cashew-nut shell, to protect the hull from sea pests. Some are mending their nets and the fisherwomen are hurriedly gathering the fish spread out to dry and taking them into nearby huts.

The sea rips and roars as the waves gather force. The waves roll and rise finally ejaculating on the beach in froth and foam. The sandpipers chase the dissolving froth, probing the sand with their long beaks like forensic experts examining a rape victim.

We plunge into the cooling waters and play around. By late afternoon, a change in the weather is discernible beyond the horizon. A cool wind begins to blow and soon turns stronger as the blue sky gets gradually enveloped in a mourning shroud of grey cloud. A pre-monsoon thunderstorm is arriving. It is too late to walk home, so we choose to take shelter in a fisherman's hut quite a few of which are built along the beach front. Nets, canoes and other implements are stored within. The thatched huts are long and narrow with low roofs and open in the front and rear to allow the wind to pass through unhindered.

The storm hits the coast heightened by thunder and lightning. Pummelled by the winds the coconut trees sway and bend low, like congressmen before the high command. The casuarinas are breaking and the sounds of tearing branches hitting the ground adds to the noise. A couple of boats, still out at sea, are being tossed around as the fishermen struggle to shore. Finally the boats hit the sand and the occupants jump out as the rain continues unabated. These are the first pre-monsoon showers of the season.

The rains finally peter off. The ground emits the strong typically earthy smell when water hits dry land. Birds on the trees are chirping merrily as the rains have brought respite even to them. Little puddles formed in the paddy fields have become bathing spots for Magpie Robins and Common Babblers which are dancing merrily around. Insects in their thousands are hovering in the air-easy picks for Green Bee-eaters, Ashy Swallow Shrikes and Starlings which seem to abound, are also enjoying the feast.

The walk back home is more comfortable as the weather has cooled and the footpath has firmed up after the deluge. One can walk easily. On either side of the beach below the sand dunes are paddy fields. Crops have been harvested, except for some, millets and lentils. The cereals are saved by the households to be consumed during the monsoon period when fresh fish and other regular food, is not available.

The next week I prefer to go alone to the beach. The fishermen are done with their fishing. The season is over. Nets are tucked in. And will lie dry, till mid-August. There is a sense of vast space. A sense of peace and serenity prevails – the type I have rarely experienced before. The sand dunes have bloomed into a vast pink bouquet of goat's feet creeper flowers. The heat and humidity is the only trespasser on this tranquil scene. As I savour the beauty, nature seems to be having a different plan. A quick change in weather looks imminent.

Before you know it, clouds twirl, thunder roars. Wind rushes, lighting flashes. Rain pours down. It is cool and refreshing. It is the second day of the first pre-monsoon showers of the monsoon season. The Arabian Sea seethes in anger. Waves crash on to the shore. Thunder struggles to be heard. Driven by ferocious winds, clouds wrinkle and swirl. The threatening sky above competes with the raging sea below. Nothing could be so frightening. And so beautiful. The winds savage the coconut trees. I again watch from the shelter of the fisherman's hut. But neither rain nor wind affects the flimsy looking hut. It stands firm against the raging elements. It rains long and hard. I reach home drenched and dripping.

"Not good at all," shouts Alberto. "The first few days of rain collect all the impurities and pollutants hanging in the air. And when you get wet these make you sick. This is the age old wisdom."

I cannot challenge his wisdom.

The showers resume the next day at the same time in the late afternoon. And with the same accompaniments.

The rains hit the tiled roof with terrific noise. As the sun dips so do the rains, a pleasant breeze continues to blow. Albano the toddy tapper who cannot play much football, comes over to remind me that it is the night of the frogs.

"Finish supper by seven-thirty," he advises.

As I gulp down dinner my friends, are outside holding torches made of dried coconut leaves. They are carrying empty gunny bags too. Accompanying Albano are Caetano, Luis and Roque. Albano is an amiable man, well loved by the villagers. He is the expert for our night out. Two other friends join us along the way.

"There has been the right amount of rain," porounces Albano as we trudge along.

The fields are murky with little pools of water. The nights hitherto silent, have with the rains, gained a life of their own. The shrill buzz of the cicadas is drowned by the croaking of the frogs. The creatures which have slumbered underground since the end of the previous monsoon are responding to the first rains of the new season. They have clawed their way out through the soil softened by water percolating down. And are merrily croaking looking for partners. Man and frog have waited for this moment. Both are out for the night. For different purposes – the frogs to mate, the men for their meat.

I just cannot believe that there could be so many frogs. The yellow creatures are everywhere almost waiting to be scooped up. They are easy to catch but difficult to hold. Their bodies are slimy and slithery. More get away from the grasp than get into the bags. Nonetheless, our bags are full in a short time due to an abundance of the amphibians.

It is now that the expertise of Albano that comes into play. The rains also bring the field crabs out. Experience and expertise is needed. And Albano has both. The crabs have claws that can snap an unwary finger into two. They have to be approached from the rear because their claws cannot turn three hundred and sixty degrees. But their telescopic eyes can.

The moment a crab sees a movement with its roving eyes, it decamps to its burrow and does not come out until the threat has moved away. For this purpose, stealth and precision is the need. Albano soon justifies his well-earned reputation. While most other friends have seen fruitless attempts with the crabs swiftly disappearing into their retreats and one or two even get clawed. Albano shows his proficiency at the grab-a-crab process. Not one escapes his claws. We spend three hours and return with two sacks full of frogs and a sack full of crabs. For me the experience is more exhilarating than the catch.

I cannot bring myself to eat a frog. Ah, but the crabs are delicious.

It is just days after the pre-monsoon showers of my first monsoon in Goa and the changes brought about by the rains are all visible. The drab grey of the soil is replaced by soothing green of emerging grasses and shrubs. The entire village seems to have moved to the paddy fields, digging, ploughing and generally doing agricultural work. No one is idle. Cattle and goats abound. One can see why the villagers were eagerly awaiting the arrival of the rains. The bounty of the rain determines the food supply of the village for the entire year. The whole atmosphere is of agro-pastoral tranquility.

Chapter 9

The Wreath

Today, as I get set to join the boys to play football, *Bhatkar* comes over and requests me to go to Margao to purchase a wreath and lay it for his dead school mate and good friend at Colva. He also recommends that I go to the flower shop called Flora at Old Market. He explicitly requests me to tell the owner that he has sent for the wreath and gives fifteen rupees towards the cost of the wreath and an amount of three rupees as pocket money to me. He provides a piece of paper with the words - *Minhas mais profundas condolencias* with his name to be written on the ribbon attached to the wreath. The funeral is scheduled for four o'clock the next day. As he leaves he calls me back and says, "How will you go? Take my bicycle when you need it. But see that you are at the house before the cortege is taken out. You may take one of your friends with you as you may not be familiar with the town."

From among the boys, José jumps up to join me on the trip to Margao, since I am looking for help, being unfamiliar with both Margao and Colva. By afternoon, after lunch on the next day we pedal off.

José does not stop at Old Market as we pass the flower shop displaying the signboard "Flora" but continues to pedal onwards. Forget Flora he says, as I point towards the shop. We pass by the Praça Jorge Barreto and turn left. He stops opposite a shop named *Bonamis* housed in a tiled structure with several shops in it. We enter and José asks for a white ribbon and a few are shown. He selects one that is expensive, costing fifty paise. The others are cheaper. We move on to the Praça Jorge Barreto and take a seat on a garden bench. He takes out the ribbon and a black crayon from his pocket, which he has brought with him. He asks me for the farewell message which *Bhatkar* has given and copies it with practiced ease in running hand, on the ribbon.

"Now where is the wreath?" I question, my suspicions aroused.

"There is no need for the wreath as you will see. You need to do nothing."

But I feel dubious.

What will the *Bhatkar* think if we play some trick on him? Will I not lose his goodwill and the chance to use the library? I say to myself. At the same time I do not want to lose my friendship with the boys.

I try to wriggle out of the tight spot I find myself in and tell him, "But the *Bhatkar* has specifically said that I must obtain the wreath from Flora and that he may check with him."

"No worries, I will take care of that," says José.

I have no choice but to keep quiet and let things take their own course.

By 3.30 pm we are at the funeral house which is not difficult to find. People dressed in mourning clothes are proceeding there and we silently follow them. The house is crowded with mourners. The body in a black coat and black tie with the arms folded on the chest holding a crucifix and a rosary, lies in the coffin. The cover of the coffin is kept outside the front door with a plate bearing his name, date of birth and death. Several wreaths lie on and around the coffin. The priest arrives, the prayers are said and the coffin taken out. There is muted crying. A family member tells someone to take the wreaths out after removing the ribbons. At this time, one or two persons pick up the wreaths and begin to take off the ribbons. José also joins them, picks up a few wreaths unties the ribbons and puts them in his pocket. Later, he gives the same to the family member standing at the door.

I assume our task is over although I still fail to understand what the hell is going on. But José insists we have to proceed to the church. It is a convention that we drop a handful of mud in the grave.

We proceed to the church which is a long way off. It is not easy to walk the coffin with three men holding each side along the narrow path. It becomes a sort of a relay as those holding the coffin, hand over charge to the next group. The cortege reaches the road after nearly half an hour where it is placed on a hand-drawn hearse. A drizzle begins. The *Pedo** pulls it to the church. The cover of the coffin is removed and kept against the front wall of the church, by the main door and the coffin taken in and set down befor the altar. The service is solemn. The young priest preaches the homily and paints a saintly picture of the dead man. "The priest is trying to send him to heaven but he may not reach even half way there" mutters the man standing by my side, to no one in particular. The man at his rear taps him on his shoulder and whispers "The priest is his nephew." The service ends with a soulful rendition of the portuguese hymn *Jesus Bendito Meu Redentor.*

After the service we move in a procession to the cemetery which is further by the side, on the other side of the road.

The coffin is lowered into the grave. Silence reigns and is only broken by the final prayers of the priest. The psalm 23 *The*

---

* undertaker

*Lord is my shepherd I shall not want"*is solemnly rendered in Konkani. It sounds so different here in Goa. The priest drops the first spade-ful of mud which falls with a thud on the coffin. The wife of the deceased gives a deep sigh. The family members join in and are then gently led to the door of the cemetery where they line up to receive condolences. The mourners gather in an orderly queue. The *pedo* fills up the grave and levels it. The wreaths are placed on top of the grave.

Now I am confused even more. The money for the wreath is still in my pocket. José sees my confusion.

"Everything has gone off well. No need to panic," he says.

"I will tell you how it works," he continues.

We ride back to the *Bhatkar*'s house and return the bicycle.

"Did Flora give you a proper wreath?" asks the *Bhatkar*.

José intervenes, "I took Ismael to Shanu who provides better wreaths. You ought to have seen the wreath. Lovely white flowers. It outshone all the other wreaths. Besides, Flora has a dubious reputation. It is said that he visits the cemeteries after funerals, collects the wreaths and recycles the flowers. So, not many patronise him." *Bhatkar* seems sceptical on hearing José but thanks him all the same.

"But you have damned Flora and his business," I tell José.

"Well the rogue deserves it. I used to supply flowers to him. He bought from me for about six months and began to pester me about the source of my supply. He refused to believe when I lied to him that my mother cultivates the flowers, claiming that these flowers do not grow in Goa. And in the end he stopped buying from me. He had got me followed and identified my source and took it over by offering a better price.

"Moreover he is a bad person known to trouble women. Everybody knows he suffers from *a weakness of the lower end*," he says in typically picturesque Konkani.

"And what is that source?" I question.

"The *pedo*, who else?" he laughs.

"But you are no better than the owner of Flora then?"

"Have I double crossed anyone?"

"So now you no longer sell flowers," I say to him.

"Why not? I am not one to give up because of a little hiccup," he quips.

"Now I have expanded my business and doing even better. You see I had a deal with three or four undertakers who after a funeral would pick up the best flowers from the wreaths and keep them for me for an agreed price. I would collect them later in the evening and deliver them to Flora early next morning at much less than the market rate. Thus I have earned for the day before Margao wakes up from the previous night's slumber. But I do not give up after Flora's stab in the back. There are thirty parishes in Salcete and around. Now I have organised myself better and formed a cartel of about twenty undertakers in the neighbouring parishes who are on my regular pay roll. It means I have to cycle a little more, sometimes Xavier or Francis also help. But earnings are more too. This time I have warned every *pedo* that if he deals directly with the florist I will expose him and the entire business will crash. I have made it clear that if I do not earn, nobody earns! They not only collect flowers from wreaths but also bouquets left at the church after nuptials."

"And whom do you sell to?"

"Shanu for one," he says with a glint in his eyes. "And almost all the others. And they do not question my source. Why should they, when the cost is much less? I have a feeling they do know my source because they also buy some fresh flowers from the wholesaler. They are careful to mix both in a wreath. And if they do not buy fresh flowers I will go out of business. After all a flower has a short shelf life and can only be recycled once."

"That is fine. But we never placed a wreath for the dead man..."

"I will tell you how it works," he interrupts.

"You must have seen there was a heap of wreaths on the

coffin and by its side. No one even has a chance to look at the individual wreaths, particularly those that are placed towards the beginning of the funeral march. The only way to know who has placed them is the name on the ribbon. The ribbons are unfastened from the wreaths before the funeral cortege proceeds to the church and kept at home. The wreaths accompany the coffin. After the initial shock of death has waned, the ribbons will be taken out and the names recorded on a book. Later the family will reciprocate when a member of the other family dies by sending a wreath. You must have noticed that I used the most expensive ribbon, which is an indication of the quality of the wreath. I consciously stayed back so that I could help in taking out the wreaths and removing the ribbons and putting them in my pocket. And I gave all the ribbons in my pocket including our ribbon to the man collecting them. Did you not notice it? That is an essential part of the ruse. Ultimately it is the ribbon and not the wreath that is counted."

After football the next afternoon, José offers to take everyone for snacks at the local teashop.

"Tell us' who offers us the treat," pipes in Antonio.

"Oh, it is João Santana Rodrigues from Colva who was buried yesterday," says José.

Everyone stands up, says a short prayer to the deceased before partaking of what is on offer. I make the payment and still get back three rupees. Everyone seems satisfied-*Bhatkar*, the deceased and we, above all. José slaps me on the back and says,

"Do you not agree that our wreath was the best?"

Chapter 10

Catching Birds

The monsoon season in Goa is drawing to an end and the boys look forward to the onset of the dry season. All of us walk and descend about a yard and a half to enter the paddy fields. It is early morning. Little ponds full to the brim and glittering like jewels on a necklace all along the margin of the paddy fields greet us in all directions. A broad bund separates the fields of Betalbatim from the fields of Calata.

A score or so coconut trees stand on the bund, each of which has nests of weaver birds hanging from the leaves. Some of the nests are elongated and shaped like oversized penes. The egg chambers look like the scrotum.

A few others are built differently and function like swings. And as the wind blows, the nests sway like pendulums. The gregarious weaver birds are noisily flying around. The females are not particularly colourful and look like the house sparrow. The males wear a bright yellow crown a brown mask, a blackish bill streaked with yellow, with underparts even more yellow and cream.

The paddy crop is ripening. It is nesting time for the birds.

The murky field is filled with ankle deep water and slush. I am reluctant to walk in but everyone else runs in unhesitatingly as if it is the most natural thing to do. The water splashes on all sides. Seeing my discomfiture, Caetano and Pedro come rushing in and pull me into the muck.

"Now, you are in it you might as well enjoy it. When in Goa, do as the Goans do," says Caetano.

Manuel climbs up a coconut tree and cuts down a leaf. The ribs of the leaf are separated from the leaflets and carefully cut to size and turned round into rings. Each of them shimmies up a coconut tree, bends a leaf towards himself, and checks whether eggs are laid or hatched in the nest. If so, he lets the leaf go. He then places the ring carefully at the opening of an empty nest so that it fits tightly in. The birds are noisily flying around as their nests are under invasion.

The boys slide down. They then take it out on me by kicking slush and mud on me. Before long we are all a mess, dripping with muck. Calm returns after about half an hour.

'Now look at the Bombay boy," they shout in unison.

The birds resting on the coconut trees one by one carefully enter their nest perhaps to inspect the damage done by the intruders. But to my astonishmant as each bird enters the ringed nest, it drops down into the fields. The birds are picked up their wings freed and are released into cages which the boys are carrying. The traumatized birds fly around the cages desperately seeking a way out.

It is an innovative way of catching the birds, which the villagers have perfected down the years. The weaver bird nests are hanging with the nest openings facing down. Once the birds enter the nest hole their wings are caught in the ring and being unable to fly the birds drop down like stones.

"You may, have twenty storied buildings and double decker buses in Bombay but can you do this in your city?" taunts Luis.

Well I had never seen anything like that.

"Be prepared for a bigger bird show later," barges in Antonio.

The same evening, we go cycling, past the Mae de Deus Church and towards Dongorim. We end up on the banks of the River Sal. The waters do not flow as the river has been bunded at Rumbde creating a wide lake to facilitate fish breeding and irrigation during the dry season.

We all dive into the calm waters, after a brief prayer at the black painted Holy Cross atop an artistically designed pedestal, standing on the bank. Tired but cooled, we step on to the banks and walk along. My friends inspect the ground below the coconut trees. Two coconut trees are selected, seemingly at random. The only difference between these two and the other coconut trees is that the ground below these trees is full of bird droppings. We ride back home.

It is a new moon night, dark and foreboding. As we cycle back to the river bank, only one of us carries a dim torch. It is nearing eleven o'clock. And some carry bamboo batons about a yard long. As I wonder what is happening, the boys ignore the two trees selected earlier and few climb the nearby coconut trees each carrying an empty gunny bag. They climb right up and squat in the palm fronds.

The action begins on the ground. Those at the bottom, bang hard with the bamboo batons on the two other coconut trees. I can hear movement in the air as herons and egrets roosting up are disturbed and fly around in the darkness, only to alight on the neighbouring trees. The birds are immediately picked and put in the gunny bags. After a good period of time, the bags with the opening tightly bound are dropped to the ground. The boys then descend to a cacophony of celebratory noises.

We cycle back, home. The next morning, all the boys gather with the gunny bags on the edge of the paddy fields near the large pond. Each bag is carefully opened, a bird picked up, its neck wrung and thrown down. By the end, almost seventy birds have been slaughtered.

The birds are dressed, feathers and the inedible parts scattered at predetermined spots in the pond so that fish continue to come to the same place and thus be entrapped and netted when needed. The catfish are immediately up, grabbing the offering.

We all march with our booty to the rather spacious house of Luis where everybody squats in the kitchen and the slaughtered birds are cut into small bits. Now, it is for the mother and sisters to do the rest. By late evening, the smell of xacuti being cooked fills the air. Caetano, who has a bakery, provides the bread and everybody eats like a glutton.

Well, I must say that nothing like this could even be imagined in Bombay and I begin to enjoy the rustic lifestyle of the boys.

Chapter 11

News report

From my childhood it has been my habit to collect old newspapers, which come as wrappings for goods purchased in the orphanage and when I have the time, I read them at leisure. Some days ago, I had collected one paper from the *Bhatkar's* house which was wrapped around dry chillies. As I tried to read it, I was forced into a bout of sneezing. So, I weighted down the newspaper by placing a stone over it, to prevent it from being blown away by the wind and kept it in the sun for the effect of the chillies to wear off.

Tonight, as I go to sleep, I pick up the paper and towards the right hand corner there is a report headlined "Conman, Wife, Son, Sentenced" which draws my attention. The hair, and a hell of a lot I have on my body, stands on end as I read the report. I draw the attention of the report to Alberto and request him to read it. But he insists that I read it aloud as the light provided by the chimney lamp is not sufficiently bright for his restored eyesight.

I read the report in The National Express as it is:

Guntakal December 10-(By our staff reporter): A father mother and son have pleaded guilty to an ingenious crime and have been sentenced to three years RI by the Judicial Magistrate First Class in Guntakal. The trio devised a near perfect trick of defrauding the railways and denying compensation and a proper funeral to victims of railway accidents. The trio, Uday Kumar, his wife Rani and son Arun, have been duping the railways for the last few years through a devious strategy and have misappropriated lakhs of rupees from the railways otherwise payable as compensation to families of victims of rail accidents. The trick used by them will do any film maker proud. It is preposterous. And they pulled it off several times with aplomb. And without raising suspicions. The confessional statement of Uday Kumar the head of the family recorded by the Magistrate and admitted by him during trial lays it bare. So it is necessary to quote it in extensio.

"It all began when I was an attendant at a morgue in Bihar. A major railway accident took place at Kalihar in March 1961 killing many passengers. The bodies were kept in the morgue. All except one body was claimed. I also read in the papers that the families of the victims were being paid compensation by the railways. The unclaimed body remained for some six months. Finally as there was no claimant it was cremated. Railways saved compensation payable to the family of one victim. So I got thinking. Why not go for it?

Dumraon railway station saw a massive accident less than a year later killing many more people than the Kalihar accident. Bodies were distributed in morgues in two or three cities. A month on, some bodies still lay unclaimed and unidentified. On my instructions my younger brother laid a claim to a body of a young girl as his daughter. The body was completely crushed and unrecognizable. The police released the body without much hassle, and were actually glad to get rid of it. A claim was put up with the railways and the compensation was promptly paid.

I resigned from my job and opened the business of following all rail accidents and claiming unidentified bodies, cremating them and staking a claim for compensation. Usually the police release the body to the claimant for a small sum without going into the nitty gritty. My wife and my son too were roped in. My brother too used to do the same thing but after he suffered a stroke he has given it up.

Nowadays, it is my son who keeps track of railway accidents wherever they take place by reading the newspapers or listening to the radio. A few days after the accident we proceed to the scene and make enquiries about the number of dead and injured. We visit the hospital and find out whether any body is lying unclaimed in the morgue. It is not difficult work as the morgue attendant provides the information and allows one to inspect the bodies for a small tip. Sometimes my son pretends to be a journalist in which case, access to the morgue is gladly provided. Usually, it is only one person who does the reconnaissance, and he makes careful note of the body with all its identification marks.

If any corpse is still unclaimed after about a fortnight, then three of us go to the police stating that our son or daughter, as the case may be, was travelling by the train and has not returned. The police check the records and take details of the missing person from us. Having done that, a police constable is deputed to the morgue with us to see whether we can identify our son/daughter.

As the morgue is opened, the body is promptly identified by the one who had come earlier,but suitably incognito. And we all start crying and mourning at the same time which goes on for quite a period. The police constable and the attendant try to console us. To avoid payment of a hefty bribe we usually dress up as poor labourers. This does the trick even better than a bribe. We then return to the police station where the police record our statements and ask for proof that we are the parents of the deceased.

As we do not have any such proof we are required to go back and bring proof which is usually a letter from the Sarpanch *of the Village. No certificate is available, unless the Sarpanch is bribed. We also obtain false school leaving certificates which are casually available for a small fee. Occasionally the body is not released unless another bribe is paid to the police.*

In the present case we learnt about the accident at Guntakal and we came over and identified the body of a young man as that of our son. On our return to claim the body with the letter of the sarpanch, and the school leaving certificate we met an elderly bearded man accompanied by younger man in the train, who helped us and even accompanied us to the morgue and the police station. They remained present till the cremation after which they went on their onward journey and we tried to return home with the record of the cremation and the letter from the police delivering the body to us.

A claim is then put up with the railways for compensation on account of the death of our son. We have obtained compensation this way in some fifteen to twenty accidents till now. Such payment is promptly made as the railway does not like to create a public dispute but a ten percent bribe is collected, nevertheless. It is for the first time ever that someone has actually laid a claim to a body after we had cremated it. But in the present case we had not reached the stage of putting up a claim as we were caught.

We deserve to be caught after several successful heists as we betrayed the trust reposed in us by the two strangers who helped us in the train. We behaved in an ungrateful manner by biting the hand that fed us. And I feel we have been punished by God for this act of treachery.

Our son Ajit here with us is an expert at opening locks. So he opened the trunk that the strangers had left in our care as they went for dinner. We found two bags full of coins inside. We emptied the bags and replaced the contents with ballast stones of similar weight, found on the tracks, restored the bags in the trunk and locked it back. We have been punished for this act of greed and thievery. The police seized the money bags from us."

It was a strange quirk of fate that the rogues were exposed. The actual parents of the dead boy turned up at the police station the day after the body was cremated.

The real parents Mohammed Aslam and his wife had been to Saudi Arabia for Haj pilgrimage on a trip financed by their son who works as an engineer in that country. Their other son was left behind in Bhopal. He decided to travel to Bangalore for a holiday with a friend but he died in the train accident. The parents were unaware of the death until their return. It took them three days to know the truth when the parents of his travelling friend, who was seriously injured gave them the tragic news. They made haste to Guntakal where they were faced with the second tragedy.

The police managed to trace the accused in the train. They were proceeding to Patna, and not to Lucknow which they reported as their home town. They had discarded the ashes without any scruples. It was a well-planned conspiracy and the plan was to mislead the police about their address too. Neither the letter of the Sarpanch nor the school leaving certificate is genuine. Under intense interrogation the accused were forced to confess.

The intriguing part of the case was the vehement assertion by the accused before the court they had two cloth bags which contained several thousand rupees in coins and which the police had seized from them at the time of the arrest. They also claimed that these coins were actually robbed by them from the Good Samaritans, who had helped them get back the body of their *son*.

The police, however, produced two cloth bags in court containing bottle caps which were attached from the accused at the time of the arrest. The court disbelieved the story of replacement of coins by bottle caps by the police. The court stressed on the fact that there was no complaint from the victims of the theft. It would certainly be the case had they been deprived of their money. The court also observed that it is routine for the accused to malign the police force.

The attached property was ordered to be destroyed if not required for any other investigation. It may be noted that the confessional statement is recorded only after the accused are transferred to judicial custody to prevent coercion by the police. The interrogation must have been really *intense* for the confession to be so detailed.

By the end of the report we are both stunned and just sit and stare unable to believe what has hit us. It takes a long period of silence for reality to sink in.

I look at Alberto who looks flummoxed. At last, I blurt out "How could we ever have trusted and helped such rogues?"

"And how could we lodge a complaint of theft when our coins had turned into stones having been witness to bottle caps turning into coins? And how could we when we had not seen the stones until we reached Goa, a day later?

"But what do we do next?"

"What else?"

"Why do we not go and lay hands on the bag of bottle caps?"

"Who knows?"

"Yes why not?"

"Do, you realise that if only the police were to carry out the same verification on the corpse that the mob did before killing my father the police could have unmasked the rogues then and there?" I wonder aloud.

The next day, we inform the *Bhatkar* that we are heading to Guntakal and will be back in a few days. The train, for once is in time as we leave early in the morning from the station. My mind is completely unsettled and I am hardly aware of the country side through which the train is passing which in ordinary course I would be intently watching especially on a bright and clear day like today.

On reaching Guntakal we check into a small hotel. After resting for some time, we go out in the town. We change our clothes suitably to look like rag pickers and collect as many bottle caps as we can from roadside soft drink vendors and put them in bags which we carry. By mid-afternoon we have collected enough caps for our bags to be filled more than half way. Alberto suggests that the police canteen may be the best place to fish for information about the case and we make our way into it. I drop my bag a bit heavily to the floor so that the caps jingle inside. There are several policemen sitting and talking loudly.

We have a simple vegetarian lunch. We see a cardboard box in the corner filled with bottle caps. The canteen man offers to sell them to us for one rupee. We pay him and put the caps in our bag. Our plan now is to ferret out how best we can raise the subject of bottle caps with the police. After lunch, we rest for a while as policemen move in and out. We are the only lay people. A tall, bulky policeman notices us and begins to question us.

"What are you two doing here?"

"We have come for lunch," says Alberto.

'What is that in your bags?"

"Bottle caps."

'What do you do with them?"

"We sell them to the factory which melts and recycles them."

"Constable take these two in, we need to investigate. There have been several thefts in our beat. It is said that the thieves come in disguise as rag or scrap pickers, survey and identify potential targets before breaking in. Let us check what these people are up to. You never know," he orders.

"But sir," pleads Alberto, "do you think we will come to the police station if we were thieves?"

"Listen, today there are thieves who will walk in and rob the police station itself in our very presence. It has happened.

And the police are made to look stupid. Take them in," he orders.

We are led inside the police station and made to sit on the floor. Our bags are taken away. By the time the tall bulky policeman reappears, it is nearing twilight. My mind is full of horror stories of police treatment of those in custody. He makes us stand up and gives several hard slaps across our faces.

"Tell the truth," he demands. "How many thefts have you committed?" He does not wait for an answer. "Lock them in," he orders the subordinates.

"Lead them before the *Saheb* when he comes."

No *saheb* comes. We spend the night in the lockup with three other detainees, sleeping on the floor.

We cannot understand them as they speak Telugu. No dinner. But the constable on duty does provide us drinking water. Next morning two constables come and take us out of the lock up. We are both kicked around, slapped, put in handcuffs and made to sit on the floor.

By eleven o'clock we are taken before the Police Inspector in his chamber. He can speak English.

He looks suspiciously at us and begins interrogating

"What is your name?"

"Alberto da Costa."

"From where are you?"

"Goa."

"Goa? And what are you doing here? Since when, are Goans collecting scrap? Goans work on the ships or distill and sell hooch in Bombay, as far as I know. First time, I have come across Goans claiming to be scrap collectors. There must be something else behind your presence here. Tell me, why are you here?"

"I have spoken the truth, Sir."

"Now, you there, what is your name?" Pointing towards me

"Ismael D'Souza from Goa."

"I cannot believe you. You do not look like scrap collectors. Either you tell the truth or I register an offence and arrest you."

"Sir I was a seaman caught in bad times after my ship

sank during the war. I was seriously injured and had lost my eyesight for many years and I lived like a beggar in Bombay. After my eyesight improved in recent time I returned to Goa only to find my house has collapsed and my property usurped by the caretaker. I am helpless. As I had no work, I took up collection and sale of bottle caps as an occupation. My partner here also helps me."

"I have heard such stories before. Give them something to eat and lock them in. We shall deal with them later." He walks away.

Two more nights we spend in custody during which we are beaten up by drunken constables. I am taken out alone on the second night. My hands and feet are tied and I am lifted up to the ceiling hanging by a rope over a pulley. I have excruciating pain all over my body and I cry out. The constables laugh out. After may be ten minutes I am brought down, provided a chair and interrogated. I have nothing new to tell them. I am back in the lockup but Alberto is not present. He is brought in an hour later visibly shaken and in pain. He has been given similar treatment.

"A bad day," I say to Alberto

"There is no such thing as a bad day. It only means one is not prepared for it."

He is in deep pain. I can see it although he seeks not to show it.

Finally we are called again before the same Officer in the morning.

"Look. We are caught up in number of unsolved crimes and we are looking for the culprits. The more the crimes the greater is the pressure against the police. Sometimes we are forced to take innocents into custody and rough them up. Without such treatment we can detect no crime. We had to keep you in, to be certain that you are not criminals. Normally after two nights the truth comes out," he elaborates.

"Constable, return their bags and release them," he calls

out.

The constable returns with our bags and delivers them to us.

As we leave, we are called back and told to hold on.

The saheb interjects and asks, "Where are those other bags of bottle caps seized from those railway crooks? Bring them here."

The constable comes back with a bag.

"Can you turn coins into bottle caps?" he asks us, and laughs out loudly. 'We came across such men sometime back. Now they are in jail." And, goes on to explain the case.

"I believe that the allegation was made because all three of them were given the *helicopter* treatment while in custody. And forced to come out with the truth. They were looking for some revenge. But they are fools. Which Judge or anyone else will believe such a story even if true? Believe me I was the Investigating Officer. We found only bottle caps in the bags."

We pretend to be unaware of any such case and laugh it off.

"Why do we not give the bottle caps attached from those railway rogues to these guys?" he says to his colleague. "At least that will be some compensation for what they suffered here."

"Should we not get rid of the 'ill omen'?"

The other nods his head, and hands over the bag to us.

"How much do we pay?'

"We have earlier on, faced false accusations because of this bag of bottle caps. Actually there are two smaller bags inside. We do not need more allegations. Take it all and go."

We thank him and move out.

"Through suffering comes salvation. The One above takes care of everything," Alberto justifies piously.

We return to the hotel in our rag picker clothes. I begin to feel that the bags have lost volume but gained weight. We are in a hurry to inspect the contents of the bags. And we feel unconcerned about our appearance. However, as we enter the hotel, the security guard is instructed to stop us by the front office.

"No place for beggars," says the security guard as he blocks our entry.

We point out that we are hotel occupants. We are allowed in after our claim is verified from the hotel register.

"Why did you dress up like beggars?" asks the front office assistant.

"To check how you deal with beggars," retorts Alberto.

Once in the room, we open the large bag given back to us by the police and find two smaller bags inside full of coins in place of the caps, to our immense joy.

"Look," exclaims Alberto as he opens the bags of bottle caps we had collected before entering the police station

"What a surprise! All these caps have also turned into coins. And the inside packing of the caps too are here. How can I doubt your story at all?"

"Oh why did we not collect more?" I react thoughtlessly.

"Do not be greedy. We must be grateful for all that we have got. How much more do you want?"

I look on sheepishly.

"We got not just our money back but also the interest as compensation for all the beatings and pain we had to bear and the trouble we had to endure," Alberto remarks happily.

As we ruminate over the happenings of the past week, Alberto feels that we should avoid giving a chance for a repeat of the previous mishap. He claims with a great deal of logic that the coins are too much of a hassle to carry around since they are bulky and weigh a lot.

But we decide to relax for some days until the pain of the third degree torture we'd received diminished before acting.

We spend the next two days just relaxing, trying to overcome the pain. On the third day we begin to separate the coins as per the denomination and make small bundles of fifty and hundred rupees each. It is decided that I stay back in the room as we cannot trust anyone, anymore. It is Alberto who takes a few bundles of coins and moves out while I continue segregating the coins and packing them in bags. He returns within three quarters of an hour to say that there is a huge demand for change. He brings more empty paper bags.

By the end of the day, all the coins are exchanged. We have a little more than forty-one thousand rupees in notes with us. We split the money between us because as we have learnt it is not advisable to put all our eggs in one basket. Moreover paper may not change into bottle caps or ballast stones!

The episode of bottle caps and coins seems to have finally ended, leaving us unimaginably richer. Hopefully, all our financial problems are in the past, as we look ahead to a more serene and prosperous life. As I had left Bombay in a hurry, it is decided that we will return to Bombay before proceeding to Goa.

"Tell me Are you not afraid that the syndicate will find you?" I ask.

"Not now. I am no longer recognisable as the beggar under their control. Besides, by now I must have been forgotten and replaced by another unfortunate. And above all, I am now able to defend myself. Moreover your name is not Inacio de Melo!"

We take the next train and we are in Bombay by late night.

Chapter 12

Bombay Exploits

Now with our pockets full we have the freedom to check in at the YMCA International, Bombay Central for a couple of days in the vicinity of the slum where I was born. The YMCA has been in the forefront of popularising the game of basketball in India. They have a top class court overlooking the dining room. Dinner is served in the hotel restaurant. A game is on, and noisy supporters are shouting and encouraging their respective teams. My eyes turn watery, which is noticed by Alberto.

"What's wrong?"

"Well nothing" I say as I try to control my sobs. Between tears, I tell him

"I am reminded of my father who used to bring me here to watch the games by sitting on his shoulders. He was, I believe in his prime, the top star of the Nagpada Neighourhood House, the most prominent basketball club in the city."

I calm down, as dinner is served. We are soon, back in our room each contemplating the events of the past year and more.

Sleep soon overcomes us and neither of us wakes up till the sun is way above the horizon. Rose ringed parakeets are noisily announcing their presence on the trees outside.

Alberto chooses to stay back as he has no friends to meet, nor any issues to settle. I proceed to Bandra to my old school where I meet the faculty and the priests who are always kind to me and because of whom I am alive and able to look forward to a successful life.

I explain to them that I am shifting to Goa with a distant relative of my mother who has been traced and thank them for all that they have done for me. I hope to see them sometime.

I then make a sort of a farewell trip to the pavement bookshop where I used to work part-time when studying for my diploma to supplement my income. The owner is happy to see me and willing to take me back as he considers me to be the best helper he has ever had. He is disappointed when I tell him of my new plans but wishes me the best towards my future.

I have to wind up my presence in Bombay. I proceed to the room I share with my friend in Andheri, collect my belongings and bid him farewell. I also invite him to visit Goa a place he had always a desire to see.

On my return, Alberto feels he could use his presence in Bombay to visit the Majorda village club as his father's old trunk lies there. As per Club rules each member is allotted space to stow his trunk within which he stores his personal belongings. The top of the trunk serves as bed. These trunks are large and sturdy. As we enter the club I can see such trunks line the walls. The club is spacious with several rooms, a kitchen and a place for prayer with an altar dedicated to Nossa Senhora da Boa Morte. A few members are present but none seems to recognize us. Neither do we recognise anyone.

We make inquiries and learn that the club secretary works at Mazagon Docks and will be back only by four in the afternoon. So we decide to re-acquaint ourselves with Dhobitalao, a familiar place for Goans.

The Jer Mahal Estate building, now old and decrepit, must have been the cynosure of all eyes in its prime. David & Co who have printed invitation cards for a majority of Goan weddings in Bombay has its spacious shop on the ground floor. And so does B X Furtado, the music people. These are a few of the Goans who have ventured into business, which is otherwise shunned by them in favour of service. As we move a little down the street, a medical clinic comes into view. Dr. Cecil da Costa reads, the nameplate. I gather that he hails from the village of Majorda.

By five pm we are back at the club as more members stream in. The secretary Luis Antonio remembers Alberto's father Basil who he informs us, died many years earlier in an accident. His wife had died a few days previously and it was said that he committed suicide as he could not face the calamities that had befallen him one after the other. His only son who too was a club member was presumed lost at sea which was the fate of many Goans during the war. As Basil died without any known living family member his funeral was performed by the club. The son's membership is defunct as fees have not been paid for two decades or more is what he says. If the son returns it can be revived.

Alberto now reveals his identity. But Luis Antonio seeks proof.

"No one here can recognise you. And you are coming after so long. And that too after you are dead! Believe me no dead man has ever come back to reclaim his membership!"

Unfortunately the medical records provided to him and when he was returned back to India as also his treatment papers from KEM hospital were with Inacio. The CDC was lost in the sinking of the ship. He only had his discharge card from KEM hospital which remained with him as Inacio did not find it. He showed it as proof of identity.

"How do we know this document relates to you? Anyone can produce any discharge card and claim it pertains to himself. Where is the identity?"

Another member intercedes and says, "Do you not remember that one Inacio had come here several times claiming to be nephew of late Basilio and had offered to pay all the fees due till his death? Who knows? This man may be a link in the chain?"

"Yes, Do you also not recall he was pleading that at least the trunk of his uncle be opened as he needed some family documents which were in his custody? It was then that he was physically pushed out of the club and told not to come back unless he had a court order? Never came back though. He might have sent these people now."

We are startled to no end at the unfolding situation but at the same time glad that the club is so protective of its member's assets and interests. As we try to convince them, an elderly member limps in, looks at Alberto for a prolonged period as if sizing him up and pointedly asks, "Are you not Alberto from Majorda?"

"Yes I am."

I am mighty relieved that finally someone has identified Alberto.

"But we all believed you were dead," says the stranger.

The ship HMT Rohna certainly sank but I survived," responds Alberto.

"That was so many years ago."

"Where have you been all these years? Why did it take you so long to return to the club?"

"I survived and fell into the hands of crooks. It is only a few months now that I have recovered to be able to look after my interests. It is a long and harrowing tale.I spent many years begging at various spots in the city."

"Your appearance reminds me of the storyline of *Nirmon* Is it based on your life?"

"What is *nirmon*?" questions Alberto.

Alberto has neither heard of nor seen the Konkani hit movie based on the life of a seaman lost at sea who returns after many years to a world that has changed. The movie was so successful that a Hindi version Taqdir was made and ran to full houses. I saw both movies. The original was better..

"Come to think of it I did notice an old beggar under that tree near Regal Cinema and every time I passed that side he reminded me of you. He was bearded and disheveled. He resembled you even in that state. At times curiosity did urge me to speak to him but since you were known to be dead I resisted the impulse," claims the stranger.

We remain silent

"But who are you?"

"I am not surprised that you do not recognize me either. I have aged and changed. I worked for the British India Steam Navigation Company in their office. And every time you returned from the ship you would bring chocolates for my children, facial cream for my wife and whiskey for me. Do you remember?"

"Oh my God, it's Patricio," gasps Alberto as he holds him in a tight embrace.

Patricio beckons the Secretary and informs him that he identifies Alberto.

"It was with sadness that we received the news of the sinking of the HMT Rohna, in the company office. So many Goans died in the tragedy. My cousin Alfred was among the dead. So many survived and even resumed their careers. I did inquire about you but none had seen you alive," says Patricio.

"For years your friends Luis Aleixo Viegas from Velim and Romano Fernandes from Cuncolim would inquire, whether there was any news about you, whenever they came to the office. The duo really missed you, one could see," says Patricio.

"Oh great. We were all on the ship as the bomb struck but lost contact in the chaos. It is heartening to know that they have survived."

"But they had a terrible time in the sea. Both floated on a plank of wood for three days and were almost dead when rescued. Luis Aleixo was injured in the ears and has gone partially deaf. Both were awarded medals for the courage displayed by them in the face of adversity."

"And where are they now?"

"I do not know. But they have both retired. I have learnt from my relatives that the sons of Luis Aleixo are successful and prominent young lawyers in Goa."

Now everyone converges around us and is keen to know about Alberto's life story from death to rebirth.

"Now is not the time, it is a long story. And I will certainly share it with you all. But not today. I have come looking for my father's trunk. I shall be glad to renew my membership and pay all the fees due and overdue. I shall be grateful if you help me urgently as I have to leave for home tomorrow."

Patricio intercedes on our behalf and they are all ready to assist us. In the course of the conversation I realise that Patricio is the elder statesman of the Club and well respected.

All the old and abandoned trunks are stacked on the upper floor we are informed. Up we go five or six of us. As we reach up the floor the room is opened. It is dark and dusty. Everyone is helpful. Finally someone says,

"It is here, the name Basilio".

Two members carry the trunk. And bring it down. The name BASILIO is scribbled on it in bold black letters. No surname.

Someone brings a hacksaw blade and struggles to cut open the lock. The trunk is opened to a musty smell. Despite the passage of time everything is immaculately packed. There is a photo of Alberto with his sister and parents affixed to the inside of the lid. Alberto bursts out crying uncontrollably on seeing it. Patricio suggests that the trunk be closed and later opened by Alberto in privacy. Alberto pays the dues and renews his club membership and also makes a small cash gift to the club. As we depart carrying the trunk Alberto tells them he will be back and they all deserve a party. For the second time we hail a taxi put a trunk in the dickey and proceed, waving to those who came to bid us farewell.

Chapter 13

Back to Goa

The next morning, before dawn we are off to VT. The booking clerk informs us there is no ticket but a dalal soon contacts us and offers two reserved seats at a premium price though. I insist on a window seat which he offers. So there we are, with reserved seats in the train.

The train passes through not unfamiliar sights. I look out of the window and notice rows upon rows of people, of both sexes squatting by the tracks, ladies with their rears exposed and their faces covered with their sari pallus, easing themselves by the tracks. And as the train pushes onwards, the reality hits me. The Indian railways may be the second longest network in the world. A fact not particularly well known is that the railway is also by far, the longest open air toilet in the world!

Soon the train gathers speed as Bombay is left behind by way of a bridge over a creek. Some strange and unhealthy stink permeates the air reminding me of the hydrogen sulphide gas which we used to prepare in our school laboratory. Gradually we leave the crowds and smells of Bombay and pass through Thane and adjacent areas. The train speeds up. I can see water bodies looking like salt pans on my side of the track. Otherwise, the country side has nothing extraordinary about it except for the marshland gleaming pink with flocks of flamingos sifting through the mud with their downward curling beaks.

The train is typical, overcrowded and the reservations become meaningless as passengers come and push themselves anywhere and everywhere. The TC apparently is in connivance with them andsimply shrugs his shoulders.

At Bhor Ghat the train starts its upward journey wriggling through tunnel after tunnel and finally reaches Khandala. The ghat is enveloped in misty clouds. Every curve in the track reveals a different panorama. The train then pulls away over a stretch of bare Deccan, landscape until we reach Miraj. Beyond Miraj, the vastness of the plateau stretches ahead. A row of green hills in the distance break the monotony. We are now into cotton territory as the train zips past fields in various stages of ripening with men, women and children picking up the cotton bolls. Somewhere along, there is a glorious stretch incorporating dramatic rock faces and a clump of evergreen trees.

Passengers begin to socialise and I can see that the compartment contains a microcosm of the country from the language and style of dress of the passengers. Nevertheless, there is camaraderie as the passengers share their food. Little children run around the little unoccupied space in the aisles. The atmosphere is jolly. A bottle of Solan No.1 is opened and soon there is whiskey-fueled merriment which almost degenerates into a scuffle, before the intervention of some ladies restores order.

I am glued to my window, as for, the first time in journeys over this track, I am light headed enough to be able to enjoy the landscape. We now enter sugarcane country with green fields on either side. Patches of vegetables, sunflowers and cereal crops also dot the land. The train blazes its way and moves from the rather bleak to the beautiful and foreboding jungles of the Western Ghats, a part of the journey I have been looking forward to. The woods are dark and green as thousands of trees struggle with each other to reach the sunlight which barely penetrates the forest floor. Lianas and tropical climbing plants entwine themselves around tree trunks in eerie loops as they reach for the sun.

We eventually arrive at the Londa junction where we have to change trains as the track to Goa is metre gauge. The next train is due only late in the evening and we have more than half a day at our disposal. There is no restaurant as such in the station but the place is served by a scruffy looking eatery just outside. We eat whatever is on offer and Alberto prefers to relax in the station.

I have never seen such luxuriant vegetation earlier and I cannot resist the temptation of moving into the jungle. I find that though Londa is not in Goa, people here are Konkani speaking and I meet a boy of my age whom I persuade to accompany me for a walk through the jungle. And off we go as he warns me against the danger of leeches and poisonous snakes, which abound in the terrain.

The forest floor is thick with decomposing leaf litter. Some of the trees are unimaginably tall. Birds can be heard singing but are not particularly visible in the dense canopy. My friend points ahead but my eyes struggle to see what he sees. As my eyes adjust to the surroundings I can see a wild boar some distance away foraging the soil. It, lifts its snout with its gleaming upturned tusks and soon goes back to its feeding. The Malabar hornbill is too big and too colourful to be missed. There are a few of them feeding on the fishtail palm, on my right, to my delight.

My new friend leads me to a water hole with soft footfalls. We wait behind a thicket. The jungle reverberates with sounds I cannot identify. A Malabar squirrel is being chased by another on a liana a little distance ahead. My friend signals me to be quiet as something comes crashing through the trees, I am scared, it may be a tiger. I have read that tigers conceal themselves near a waterhole ready to pounce on an unwary creature come to quench its thirst.

But it is a Sambar deer which stands regally at the edge of the water hole for a moment, with its antlered head held high and takes a look around, spreads its legs before bending down and dipping its head in the water. Thirst quenched, it once again stands still and raises its head majestically, surveys the surroundings and walks away serenely. It is my *Monarch of the Glen* moment. My trip has been fruitful. We walk back to the station and I bid farewell to my new friend and tip him a small amount despite his reluctance and press him to accept. He leaves happily.

The train finally arrives well in time for us to descend the ghats in daylight, another part of the journey I had been looking forward to. The train gently trundles out of Londa in a cloud of misty smoke puffed up by the steam engine, and after a while it halts at a small station Senaulim on the top of the section of the hills called Braganza ghats. The Dudhsagar waterfalls are formed by a river tumbling down the Ghats. The waters merge into the River Mandovi that meanders around the hills of the hinterland and straightens through the plains of coastal Goa.

I am excited to be at the falls as the train descends slowly but noisily. I can hear the roar of the falls over the noise of the train much before the falls become visible. The falls come into view as the train crosses a little bridge midway below the falls.

Happily, the train halts to enable the travelers to have a closer look. The waters rappel down the western face of the ghats frothing and foaming into a *an ocean of milk* which its name Dudhsagar signifies. The waters skip from ledge to ledge before hitting the bottom a thousand or more feet below. The foamy white falls are obscured in some places by the thick green foliage which seems to overlap the falls at various spots. It is truly a sight for the gods and I hope to visit Dudhsagar again at a more leisurely pace to explore or to just laze.

Shortly, the falls and the ghats are behind us as the train descends into the plains of Goa. The train stops at Collem. We learn that there is some trouble with the engine and the train may be inordinately delayed. We are not surprised as delays and breakdowns are not strangers to our railways. So I have a few hours to wander around. Alberto prefers to lie down. We are about seventy yards above sea-level and some Forty-five miles from the sea. Behind the train, the great wall of the Ghats which we have just descended, rises up in all its luxuriance. The descent from the Ghats is steep with little waterfalls glistening in the sun in every direction with the waters then emerge as streams that make up the bulk of the waters of the Zuari-Mandovi river systems. The silhouette of the mountains in the rays of the setting sun is vivid and impressive.

Chapter 14

Tracing the House

We finally arrive home relieved, happy and rich. Before going to bed the trunk is lifted and placed on the table. I unlock it and lift the cover and step aside leaving Alberto to examine the contents.

Once again he begins to sob as he unpacks the contents. I leave him alone. He finds his father's clothes and a dress of his mother. He hugs them and cries loudly. As he calms down, he unravels a cloth bundle. Wrapped inside are gold ornaments. Alberto begins to sob again. There are two necklaces, several rings, ear-rings, chains, bangles, bracelets for amulets, brooches and a tie pin.

He picks up a necklace studded with rubies and says, "This one is from my grandmother and is a family heirloom. She used to love to wear it. And this one came as part of my mother's dowry. This is a simple necklace. My mother's parents were poor."

A few other items are uncovered. And in another cloth bag neatly packed, are documents which reveal them to be a sale deed. "So that's it," says Alberto. "The documents are here." He then finds several family photos and a roll of paper. He holds the roll and cries again.

"My father's *Nolli**￼ he gushes.

His mother is fair and good looking. But his sister is pretty, extremely pretty.

"Boys were falling for her from all over. I do not know whom she married," he says. "Hope she is happy. Maybe I will find her someday."

"I must thank the honesty of our club members. That no one touched the trunk for twenty-five years. And those rogues whom we had helped had broken into my trunk within half an hour. What a contrast. I believe being Goan makes a lot of difference."

"But the man who sold you to the beggars syndicate was Goan too. Was he not?" I prod gently.

"Oh, he was. But there always are black sheep. I am referring to Goans as a community," he justifies.

The next morning we move over to see the *Bhatkar* who as usual is sitting in the balcão with a cup of black tea which he sips as he reads through *A Vida* a Portuguese newspaper. We sit for sometime as he glances over the headlines. He keeps the paper aside and Alberto hands over a packet of tea powder,roasted grams and peanuts purchased in Dhobitalao. Alberto then provides the sale deed to him. It is in Portuguese. The document is very well preserved. He goes through it carefully. And then says.

"Perfect. The title is clear. Now I can also place the locality where your house is, why don't you go and trace it?"

"Well, we are not so familiar with the village. Can you recommend someone who can help us?"

"Alright we will proceed to the area and make local inquiries. Tomorrow, early morning."

We find ourselves trudging a regular pathway proceeding straight ahead in front of the house of the *Bhatkar*. People are

---

* a word used in Goa to refer to a sailor's CDC

up, children marching to school others running for the bus or train. All raising clouds of dust. Our walk is relaxed. Little whitewashed crosses lie along side. We reach the rail tracks and crossing over, *Bhatkar* stops to talk with a villager, tending goats. Soon we cross a katcha road which I ascertain is the same that runs parallel to the railway line further down.

"That is the chapel dedicated to *São Roque* the patron saint of the village of Calata," explains the *Bhatkar*, as he points to a large whitewashed structure to our right.

"Chapels dedicated to *São Roque or São Sebastião* are found in nearly all villages as these are saints against disease and pestilence. These were built in the old days when diseases like small pox, TB and plague were rampant and modern medicines did not exist. A prayer to these saints was believed to bring in a cure. And was the only remedy whether it worked or not. The discovery of vaccines and other medicines has markedly reduced devotion to the saints," he adds.

We reach a broad bund with paddy fields on either side. On one side of the bund is a little cottage with an old man wearing a hat sitting outside. *Basilkinho* calls out *bhatkar*. Both talk for some time. We turn right and enter an oval shaped coconut grove standing alone in the midst of paddy fields like an island, two metres above the surface of the paddy fields.

There is an unoccupied mud walled house with country tiled roof with its door shut, towards one end. A cool wind blows across.

"We are on the right track," exclaims Alberto suddenly.

"Somewhere nearby there is a large pond where we would swim and frolic during the May vacations on our visits home. I cannot forget this isolated grove as, after a swim we came here for tender coconuts. Once we nearly got caught when the owner happened to come by. A friend who had climbed half way up a tree jumped down and sprained his leg. But we escaped."

Bhatkar smiles wryly.

We move out of the grove and end up on another bund.

After sometime Albert exclaims again.

"That is the pond."

"This is Toleabund pond," says *Bhatkar*.

The pond is nearly full. Lotus and lily plants are struggling to break the surface. A few herons and egrets are perched on the trunk of a coconut tree fallen into the water. Some coots and cormorants are swimming or diving in the water. I can see a single darter swimming with its body under water and head projecting above, giving it the distinctive look of a snake. We continue to walk. Ahead of us is a man carrying a wooden plough across his shoulders.

"Marcelino," *Bhatkar* shouts out to him.

The ploughman stops and waits for us. He is bald not very tall and looks elderly. He greets *Bhatkar* and both of them begin to talk. The plough is kept by the side and Marcelino calls us to follow him. We walk along another sandy pathway until we reach near the paddy fields on the other side.

The whole stretch is one large coconut grove with ridges separating different private holdings. Some are well tended. Others look abandoned. Marcelino points to a plot quite large with a barbed wire fence around and ruins of a house and a well in it. Several young coconut trees, a few mango grafts a jackfruit tree among others are seen in the land which looks well-tended.

"That is the land," he points out

"The house collapsed many years ago due to neglect. Basilio is believed to have died in an accident at Bombay soon after his wife had died. Nobody knows for sure."

"But who has put the fence?" inquires *Bhatkar*

"You know him *Bhatkar*. It is that Damião Sequeira from across over there in Guirim, the oil press man whom you had earlier helped when he was in serious trouble," answers Marcelino.

"Why has he put the fence?"

"He is the god-child of late Basilio and was the caretaker of the property earlier. Now he claims to be the owner."

"Can you give him a message to see me? Do not tell him why."

"I will."

Two days later *Bhatkar* calls us over. As we enter the balcao a man perhaps slightly younger to Alberto is seated there and talking with *Bhatkar*.

"Alberto, this is Damião your father's godchild. He was as you must be aware caretaker of the property. He says he has developed the property over the last quarter century and is now the owner. You may talk to him," *Bhatkar* says.

Damião remembers him but Alberto does not seem to.

"I have planted trees, fenced and invested money all these years on the property. How can you come after so many years?"

"Well I will recompense you for your expenses and the trouble you have taken" says Alberto.

"Will not do, the property is mine after all these years"

"Have you not earned by selling the produce?"

"Not much, the property is only productive since the last few years. Before that I had to put in so much of money. And now that the land is productive you have come to claim it. Do you now want to enjoy the fruits of my labour?"

"Did we authorize you to develop the property?"

Damiao stands up and angrily challenges. "Do what you can. I will not surrender the property. Go to court if you must. I will see who takes away the property from me!" He stomps away

"What do we do?" Alberto thinks aloud

"It is for you to decide," the *Bhatkar* tells Alberto. "You may have to consult a lawyer and get an opinion," he adds.

"It is my father's property purchased with hard earned money, why must I let it go? My father will want me to take a stand. I believe he must have had a role in protecting the documents all these years and leading me to them. I owe it to him to recover the property. I had a friend on the same ship which was sunk but he survived. He is from Velim. His sons are lawyers I have learnt. Maybe I can contact them."

"Why not? A good idea. The lawyers may have empathy with you," says *Bhatkar*

Later at home, Alberto has second thoughts and says, "I know that in Goa the Portuguese law is still applicable. It may be better to engage a senior lawyer trained in Portuguese law rather than a young and fresh lawyer."

Next day we are back to the *Bhatkar* and explain the situation to him.

"Can you suggest a good lawyer versed in Portuguese law?"

"Certainly. I have this friend in Nuvem, a highly reputed lawyer. If you wish I will introduce you to him."

And so it is decided to proceed to Nuvem later in the afternoon.

As we walk back I say to Alberto, "But this Damião is a Goan."

"So what?"

"But he has grabbed your property. And you proclaim Goans are honest!"

He laughs as he adds, "We Goans are known for our honesty. Even the British hired Goans as trusted employees throughout their colonies in India and East Africa because of this trait, even though Goa was not part of the British Empire. But let me add, Liberation is having its effects. Now maybe we are joining the national mainstream!"

He simply cannot countenance any anti-Goan comment.

The same evening we proceed to see the lawyer at Nuvem. *Bhatkar* accompanies us. We cycle up the steep slope near the Nuvem church and soon turn right. The lawyer is quite tall, standing out in the verandah of his office, which is an extension of his residence. He is whistling. On seeing *Bhatkar*, he waves out and calls him in. They speak in Portuguese for some time. Alberto requests *Bhatkar* to explain the facts, which he does.

The sale deed is given to the lawyer. He calls us after two days.

It is a sultry day as we pedal up the climb again. *Bhatkar* declines to accompany us.

"Now it is your work to take care of your case. I have done my bit and provided you with a good lawyer. You must be on your own," he says.

The lawyer questions Alberto on various aspects and takes notes. He asks for the death certificates of Basilio and his wife and the birth certificate of Alberto. These are essential to establish that original owner named in the sale deed is dead and that Alberto is his legal heir, in order to sustain a suit. The lawyer then speaks: "You have a foolproof case; your title is clear with inscription and matriz in your father's name. I expect him to come out with a defense of adverse possession and limitation. If we can overcome limitation, we are through. Please do get the death certificates of your father and mother and your birth certificate.

"I was born in Bombay and my parents died there to, so we may need a little time to get the certificates,' says Alberto.

"You may take your time. No need to hurry. But you may not get a birth or death certificate as registration of births and deaths is not compulsory in Bombay. Your baptismal certificate or school leaving certificate will suffice. You may get the burial certificate of your parents from the church."

We deposit the fees. We are called back after we obtain the required documents.

"I will draft the plaint and keep it ready. You may read it after which changes, if required, may be made. It will have to be verified before being filed," concludes the lawyer.

Now the burial certificate and the baptismal certificate invite another trip to Bombay. This time, we choose to travel by bus. The trip is easier on time but harder on the body. We start before sunset and darkness embraces us as we cross the Goa borders at Dodamarg. The road is potholed, the bus lurches and rolls. Sleep comes in fits.

We arrive in the city as it begins to open. We proceed to the club. Fortunately the treasurer is in. He locates the book with the names of members with the date of their death endorsed in the margin. Basilio died on fifth January 1944. We proceed to Antonio de Souza High School (ANZA)at Byculla. The records older than ten years are confined to the record room. We file an application for leaving certificate of Alberto who had studied up to class four. We are called after a week, too long a period for us.

We move on to the St Michael's Church, Mahim where the clerk easily traces the baptismal record of Alberto as his birth date was known. We obtain a copy and proceed back to the club. Here we meet our old friend Patricio from whom we learn that the final rites of Alberto's parents were performed at the Our Lady of Health Church, Versova.

We choose to stay overnight at the club. We take around a dozen members present, for dinner to Bastani & Co. a popular restaurant close to the club. We have a good time, particularly Alberto who recounts the old days at the club. Back at the club more members have come in. All are keen to know the story of Alberto which he narrates dramatically. Every word is gulped down attentively.

The next morning we are off to Versova where we attend the eight o'clock mass. Later we call on the parish priest who is an East Indian and quite co-operative. He directs the clerk to trace the death certificate urgently. The church records as we notice are systematically maintained. Since we had the date of burial, the certificate is easily traced. He has to go through records to trace the burial certificate of Alberto's mother as we do not know the date of her death. But we mention it is the same year. It is soon traced. She had died a few days earlier to him. We thank the parish priest and leave. We arrive in Goa the next day.

We are back at Nuvem. We hand over the certificates to our lawyer. Three days later the suit is filed.

Chapter 15

A *house* of *our own*

Our financial position having appreciably improved, Alberto is obsessed with the idea of buying a house or buying, a plot and building one. However, his first choice is to buy a house so we could immediately shift in. We make enquiries over the weeks. We are shown a house at Nuvem but it was not up to the mark being old and in need of complete renovation if not reconstruction. Another house at Utorda is embroiled in some dispute.

Someone mentions to us that *Bhatkar* would be the ideal person as he has access to 'everyone and everything' in the words of a villager. So we speak to the *Bhatkar* and he mentions that there is a friend of his in East Africa whose children have migrated to Canada and do not plan to return to Goa. The owners therefore wish to sell the house situated at Chaul a short distance away. He says that he has got the keys to the house and we could have a look.

Later in the evening, we walk to the house, accompanied by Bosteão the local carpenter. The medium sized house has a nice get up with a large balcao and a verandah on one side. The house looks well kept and is enclosed within a compound wall with a land area of perhaps seven hundred square yards.

The door is opened and the mouldy smell of a house that has remained closed for long, greets us. The house has strong whitewashed beams and rafters. The roof is quite high. The house is airy with an entrance, a sitting room, kitchen and dining room, three bedrooms and a bathroom. The toilet as is the norm in Goa is detached from the house.

The *Bhatkar* conveys that the title is clear since he was involved in the drafting of the sale deed by which the plot was originally purchased and had confirmed the title himself.

Alberto exclaims, "Wonderful. Precisely what I have been looking for. I hope the price is right."

The *Bhatkar* says he has not discussed the price with the owners and does not plan to do so as he does not wish to get involved in the negotiations. However, he provides the address of the owner in Nakuru, Kenya and requests Alberto to write a letter mentioning that he has shown him the house.

Alberto receives a reply to his letter where the landowner states that he is due to come to Goa in a few months and the deal could be finalised then. So the matter rests until the arrival of the landowner.

Nearly a year later we are the owners of the house. The vendor Honofre Miranda has worked as a tailor in Nakuru for some forty-five years. His children have immigrated to Canada following the independence of Kenya. He has sold his tailoring business as his son insists on his joining them in Canada.

Both husband and wife plan to travel to Toronto via UK where his younger brother has settled. He will fly to Canada after spending sometime in Kent with his brother as he feels he may not get to see him again due to his advancing age. It is agreed that they will continue to live in the house till they complete their travel formalities. We take over the house after they leave.

Now that we have acquired a house, we are comfortable and relaxed. *Bhatkar* has become a friend and often visits us. He is a great raconteur and vastly knowledgeable.

But today as we are sitting in the balcao of the *Bhatkar*, a man approaches him. He wants *Bhatkar* to translate some documents from Portuguese to English. He speaks about a property which he has been entrusted to sell and he has to provide a marketable title. Alberto listens carefully and appears to size the man up. At home Alberto looks a disturbed man. He paces up and down the house and is in a mood that I have never seen him. After sometime he sits on the balcao in silence. I prefer not to disturb him and go out to play as Antonio and Caetano are waiting outside the gate for me.

I find Alberto in the same silent mood which persists till after dinner when we go to our rooms. I can see that the stranger has triggered some memory. He opens up over breakfast, and says he is almost certain that the stranger is the same person who had sold him out to the beggars syndicate and disappeared. He as put on some weight but hisvoice is the same and his eyes are unmistakable. The next day we meet the *Bhatkar* again and Alberto casually asks him who the stranger was.

"Oh he is Pobres D'Souza from Nuvem a sort of real estate agent but a dubious one," is the response.

"But you better not have dealings with him. He is an unsavoury character," volunteers the *Bhatkar*.

For the next few days Alberto is inseparable from his bicycle. For days, we cycle through Nuvem, a rather big village, until we find Pobres at a tavern in Guirim. We enter the tavern, order a drink. Pobres is ignored. I order a soda. We sit until Pobres leaves. We pay and leave too. We follow Pobres as he cycles. We see him enter a house. We continue to ride ahead and turn back only after a few minutes to avoid suspicion. "I did not want to publicly acknowledge him and that's why I ignored him," says Alberto.

"I am pretty sure he is Inacio in Bombay and Pobres in Goa. Now that I know where he lives I can inquire further."

Chapter 16

Summer Holidays

We're all going on a summer holiday
No more working for a week or two.
Fun and laughter on our summer holiday,
No more worries for me or you,
For a week or two......

That is the sound of Bombay. And Goa is not too different. Only here, we have decided to go from the sea to the hills. And with me are all my friends from the football team, twelve of us in all, singing off tune but enjoyable all the same. The song sounds so appropriate for Goa. Cliff Richard has a real connection with the people of the land. His great, great grandmother Emeline Ribeiro was a Calcutta-settled Goan. Her great nephew was a student at my school and took pride in the link, although the singer himself never acknowledged him.

The *Bhatkar* has offered us a holiday home for a few days by the side of the spring at Belloy, Nuvem. However, Alberto insists on his coming with us.

"Semi wild boys cannot be trusted alone in the wilderness," he says.

Early morning we cycle it out to Belloy. It is a neat little cottage used only during the summer vacations.

The first day of our holiday, we charge out to the hills, José as usual is at his intrepid and adventurous best leading the charge. Narrow pathways lead up to the hill. Thorny bushes spring up everywhere. Already, Caetano is bruised by the thorns. Up and up we go and in an hour's time, we are at the crest of the hill. Alberto straggles in, slow but steady. The view from the top is stupendous. The Arabian Sea spreads out far, beyond the paddy fields and the coconut groves. The white sand beach, the blue sea and the frothing waves glimmer under the rays of the sun. A strong wind tempers the impact of heat and humidity.

By mid afternoon, we are back at Belloy. The water of the spring flows down and accumulates into a pool where we jump in and swim. The spring is crowded, so we wait till most people have moved away leaving the spring at our disposal. We then rush in and take a cool and refreshing bath as the water drops from a height

Tired and hungry we rush back to our cottage where the cook, specially engaged for us, has prepared hot and steaming food inviting us to hog. Our afternoon exploits result in long afternoon naps for all of us. Alberto advises us to take care and decides to return home. Perhaps he feels out of place among us boys.

We wake up past four o'clock and move towards the house of Agostinho whose Urrak is considered the very best in Goa. We slowly climb the hill upon which Agostinho lives. He welcomes us and takes us around his still, meticulously explaining every little detail.

"This," he points towards a large rock, "is where we extract the juice from the cashew apples. We have hollowed up the rock to carve out a two feet deep basin."

It is full of ripe cashew apples. He summons his son and requests him to demonstrate to us how the cashews are crushed. The son washes his feet and climbs the rock and into the basin. He begins to crush the cashews with his feet and the juice flows through a connecting bamboo pipe into an earthen vessel kept at a lower level.

The juice is then transferred into a larger earthen tub.

"And this is the *codem* as he points towards the earthen tub. "The juice will ferment in it for a period of three days for the best product," he continues. "But nowadays the tendency is to make quick money and in many cases the fermentation period is cut short and the result is poor quality urrak."

"And here is the *bhann* where the fermented juice is boiled." He points to a large nearly spherical earthen pot with its mouth sealed shut and placed above a fireplace at a reclined angle. Wooden logs are burning underneath.

"The spirit that evaporates is collected in a smaller earthen pot immersed in water where it cools into liquid. And this is a *lavni*." He points to a pipe of bamboo which connects the *bhann* to the condensing pot. The water is replaced periodically as it absorbs the heat from the pot holding the steaming liquor.

He goes on to explains to us, "Urrak came to be distilled in Goa in the mid-eighteenth century through European monks who missed their wine. The monks modified the wine making process replacing the grapes with cashew apples. Urrak thus is an international drink with ingredients and expertise from the world over."

The cashew, he notes, was introduced into Goa from Brazil by the Portuguese and was planted on the hill sides to bind the soil and prevent erosion. "The trees proliferated and today it is difficult to believe that they are not native. The cashew apple went waste until *urrak* was discoverrd. *Urrak* has Brazilian fruit, European distillation process and Goan labour and bears the name of Potuguese royalty. Can anything be more international? Do you know how the name *Urrak* came about?"

He proceeds to answer the question himself without waiting for a reply. Actually none of us had a reply.

"The monks who distilled the first drink liked it much because of its smoothness that it came to be called the queen of drinks. Being a new product the drink had no name. A priest then suggested that it may be named after some Portuguese queen. The suggestion was approved and the drink came to be called as *Urraka* after the daughter of the first king of Portugal, who had married the king of Leon. The priest who distilled the first drink hailed from Leon in Spain. And so he named the drink after the earlier queen of his homeland.

The name not only has stuck but has travelled to the South of India where *Urrak* has become *Arrak*, like the mango Afonso has travelled north to Ratnagiri and become *Apus*. When *Urrak* is further distilled you get a more potent drink called *feni*."

"Where did you get all this information from?" I ask, keen to know more.

"Well, I have seen eighty monsoons. Thunder and lightning frighten me, no more. And all these years, I have spent with the Salesians. We were eight siblings. Poverty was the presiding deity of our house. My father good man that he was, he could not bear to see his children hungry. A brother tended cattle for a *Bhatkar* in Verna. Sister was a maid in Cansaulim. And lucky I, landed with the Salesians. And they were mostly Europeans. And they made a man out of this little tribal boy.

"Many years passed since I went to live with the Salesians in Quepem. As years went by I met Florina from Ambaulim fell in love and married her. Many years I lived there but my heart was in these hills here where I was born. I purchased this land from my *Bhatkar* and set up my still.

"Everything I know, I owe to the Salesians. They were patient. And they were scrupulous. The art of distilling *Urrak* I learnt under their tutelage, every little detail. And if you wished to have knowledge you had to watch them work and listen to them. Silently and honestly. And I did watch and I did listen to them. That's where the knowledge has come from. Today I can speak Portuguese as fluently as anyone can.

In these lovely hills, seasons whistle through the trees as I wait for the final call. Here I was born and here I will die with the scent of the hills accompanying me to the grave," he says with no hint of sadness.

We climb down as the sun sets, carrying a few bottles of Urrak. Alberto has cautioned us against drinking to excess. Back in the cottage, after another dip at the spring, we spend the time playing cards and backgammon. The next morning we are back at our exploits in the hills. As we return in the afternoon, José reveals that he has a trick up his sleeve and if it works, we could be in for a feast the next day.

Later José walks down to the highway to the shop of Mangaldas where he buys a bunch of bananas. Earlier in the hills we had noticed big broad pathways carved out by cattle and used by humans too. As against these, there are very narrow ways tunneled through the bush, manifestly made by wild boars, porcupines, pangolins and other smaller creatures. Hence the route of the wild boars could be easily identified, something which José with his keen sense for detail had also noticed.

As the last rays of the setting withdraw from the hills, we follow José as he treks up. He stops part way and places the bananas in a corner by the pathway made by wild boars. We move away to avoid any human scent drifting over. We return around ten pm and we can see some wild boars devouring fallen cashews. As we look closely we find the bunch of bananas has disappeared. One big wild boar is lying down about a hundred yards away. We throw some stones and the other creatures run away. The boar keeps sleeping, we approach it and we use a rope brought by José to tie the legs and also the snout of the slumbering boar. We then hog-march down with Caetano and

Roque abreast and myself and José holding the rear end of the pole. It is heavier than I had anticipated it would be.

We drop the creature behind the kitchen, fetter a rope around it and tether it to a tree.

By early next morning, we notice the boar has woken up and is making loud grunts struggling to escape. It is too big for us to handle by ourselves. So we call upon Agostinho who comes down with his son and a few other villagers who cannot believe that we could simply catch a boar this size and bring it down the hill and tie it too. They are astounded and wish to know how we did it. We all point towards José, but he remains mum.

We make a deal with the villagers. It is agreed that they will slaughter the boar and the meat will be shared. They go and return with machetes and knives. They are quite adept at the slaughter and within two hours it is all done. They merrily go back carrying chunks of meat. We help the cook prepare our lunch and dinner. As the meat is too much for immediate consumption parts of it are roasted and parts salted to be carried home.

After the sumptuous meal no one is in a mood for another trek to the hills. Everyone except me prefers a dip at the spring. I have had my eyes set on a distant hillock for a solo run. I cannot miss the opportunity. A gradual climb and I am soon on the top. I gaze westwards across bare and brown paddy fields and over a canopy of coconut trees, the Arabian Sea spreads out far to the horizon and beyond. The hill is set in Pateapur with a spur jutting out towards Verna. One can observe rich and varied plant life with tall trees cohabiting with smaller plants and bushes.

Stretching out before me in the east, are further rows of smaller hills. A flock of black headed Ibis fly over the hill with their legs trailing behind. Close by in the bushes, the red vented and red whiskered bulbuls are flitting around. A red jungle fowl flies away as I am about to stamp on it, leaving behind a clutch of eggs untended.

I have carried with me Fr. O'Brien's old pair of binoculars

given to me as he left for Ireland telling me to put it to good use. Here I am, miles away from Bombay following the priest's advice. I climb up a little rise in the hill where grass, and vines now wilted by the scorching heat, abound.

As I inch forward through the entangled vines I can see a deep chasm created by a seasonal stream, parched at this time. The waters of the hill, flow through the channel and join a stream which connects to the River Sal. The chasm is not too deep but the bank on which I stand, drops steeply. I cannot climb down. Butterflies flitter around.

I head down along the edge of it until it narrows and comes to a spot where the chasm is forded by wooden logs laid across. I cross over to the other side. It has been a tiring walk. I rest in the shade of a copse of teak trees.

Further down, the vegetation is greener than the side I have left behind. I move forward and realise that a little rivulet still holding water flows through it and greenery engulfs it on either side. A little upstream is a spring flowing from inside a vertical cliff, which will become a roaring waterfall during the monsoons for a brief period as can be discerned from the wide gorge carved into the sides of the hill.

Kites glide in the sky on thermals. I identify the Brahmini and Pariah kites at sight as these are quite common raptors. And they remind me again of Fr. O'Brien who mentioned that birds are named on the basis of their principal characteristics.

The pariah is a dark grey-brown bird with unkempt feathers. It thrives in or near rubbish dumps. It is essentially a scavenger. Pariah is a scavenging caste in India at the lowest end of the social scale. The bird came to be named as pariah due to its scavenging habits.

The Brahmini kite is a handsome royal looking, chestnut brown bird interrupted by an off-white head, neck and breast. The bird is also known to be very cunning and is detested by housewives. It can swoop down and scoop up barnyard chicken, scraping for food with the mother hen and clean up the coop in no time at all. The handsome looks and cunning behavior led to it being called the Brahmini kite, I imagine!

By the time I return to the cottage, the sun is playing hide and seek with the clouds on the horizon. The rest of the boys are all at the cottage, boisterous and rowdy as usual. Our adventure in the hills has been tiring but invigorating and educative.

As we get set to return home, something inside, insistently urges me, to investigate the hills after nightfall. I broach this idea with my friends who seem thrilled at the prospect and clamour for it, with great gusto. A couple of them however, are a bit wary as they have heard of tigers and leopards lurking in the woods, at night. After a brief discussion, we settle to seek the advice of Agostinho. Contrary to what I was anticipating, the old man is all for it and agrees to trek up with us along with his sons. He is clearly taken up by our adventure, with the boar

"Since you have climbed that hill," he points towards the right "I suggest we climb this one." He points to the opposite side. We begin to trudge up. The sun is still above the horizon. The old man shepherds us through a gully with steep sides, cut into the hill by gushing rainwater. A fig tree growing behind the periphery has attracted a flock of grey-fronted pigeons gorging on its fruits and whistling merrily. The path climbs steeply after a distance, at which point, steps have been roughly hewn into the flank that permits us an easy ascent up the slope, leading to a winding cattle track through lush green woods. The tinkling of bells and a rising cloud of dust, alerts us to an approaching herd of cattle. The old man steps aside as he says, "It is their right of way. Our day has just begun; theirs has come to an end". We follow him. He pats a bull with a broken horn that has a long healed scar running down his back. Our Raja, he calls him. "He fought a leopard and survived just a few yards from here" he says and adds "About six months ago. He lost only a bit of his horn, which got stuck in the side of his adversary and broke off. The hide on his back clawed by the brute, has healed well." We all turn stiff. "Let's go back" murmurs João backed by Santan. "No need to be afraid" says old man, "Have I not survived eighty years on these and other hills facing and overcoming greater dangers? If you fear, you are lost. Let's march on," he demands. Everybody falls in line.

Up and up we troop. The old man is far more agile than the whole lot of us, notwithstanding his age. Experience has made him surefooted, so too his sons. He canters, where we struggle and bumble. We round the last bend, panting and grasping for breath. He is already up there, displaying no effect of the uphill climb. The top is a plateau, not a peak as I thought it would be.

"This," says the old man is *Kallu* pointing to a black dog and "that" pointing to a white dog with a big black splotch on its head is *Chandu*. Both dogs had charged up the hill far ahead of us and were squatting on their hind quarters with their tongues hanging out. As soon as they see the old man and his sons they dance around fawning and jumping about as if to say look here, we beat you to it!

We admire the thin sliver of the river Sal, robbed of its waters for irrigation and now looking like a streamlet. It will turn into an urecognisable and raging torrent overflowing its banks, weeks hence, after the monsoons break out. On the other side in the far distance a broad river flows languidly westwards, to ultimately merge with the Arabian Sea, a few miles downstream.

"That is the mighty Zuari, the longest river in the land. Its waters are tidal, hence saline, and not useful for irrigation. The river never dries up, unlike the Sal. The river was deep, very deep in my childhood. None could fathom its depth even a few yards from the bank. I know, because in the old days, a group of us would swim across, but always a canoe each had to row behind and ahead of us, just in case. Earlier ten barges could ply abreast. Today, only a narrow channel is navigable so all barges queue up one after the other, like people at a ration shop. And when the tide is real low no barge can ply at all. The river bottom has silted due to open cast mining upstream. The mining rejects left by the pitheads, are carried by the swift flowing streams that originate in the hills and eventually join the river. The heavy silt settles at the bottom. The mines provide work for us during the slack season. Half of our village empties during the mining season. My parents too have worked in the mines," proclaims Agostinho.

"Such a thing never happened in the old days though, when laws were strictly enforced and no violation was tolerated. Everyone, the mine-owners, the workers and government employees respected the laws. Order and discipline prevailed. The mining rejects were properly stacked with no scope for spillage. Today everything is haphazard." The sadness in his voice is evident as he bemoans the days gone by.

The slope of another hillock a long distance away, is hazy so I peer through my binoculars and discover a giant staircase carved into the slope, set alight by the rays of the setting sun. The challenging environment has been conquered by chipping away at the slopes and creating geometric patterns of flat terraced fields. The rain water flowing down is tamed and channelised for proper distribution. The terraces are centuries old and the work is expertly executed to prevent mudslides. But elsewhere we see the not so subtle intrusion of modern machinery with reckless cutting of slopes.

As the sun dips below the horizon, shadows step up the hills. Diurnal birds and animals are returning to their roosts. Their nocturnal counterparts are stirring for their night out. It's another moment I have been looking forward to. The distant howl of jackals and hyenas sends fear coursing through us. But the old man and his sons show no signs of fright. That is encouraging.

"But if the leopard or tiger snicks in how do we know?" inquires Santana the most timid of the group.

"No chance with *Kallu* and *Chandu* here," responds the

old man

"But the leopard will snuff them out with a swipe of the paw," fears Santan.

"Look here" the old man responds. "These dogs can smell a tiger or leopard from hundreds of yards away. The moment they sense a presence they will start barking. The leopard or tiger is a stealth hunter. It crawls silently and jumps on the back of its victim, rarely the front, unless surprised. Thus when the dogs bark, we too join in raising a racket. See this, he points to an empty kerosene can he has carried along; we bang it loud with a stick. The creature slinks away."Our fears are allayed.

We accompany the old man up a rock which rises above the surroundings. It provides a vantage point, with an all-round view. "From here you can get a proper view. If you keep quiet, an unwary creature may land right before you. So remain silent and watch," directs the old man. Santana looks disturbed on hearing him. All is quiet except for the alarm cry of a red wattle lapwing, as it flies overhead. Twilight hurries away as we eagerly take up comfortable positions. Stars begin to spy on us through breaks in the cloud cover. A strong wind drives away the clouds revealing a quarter moon, but more clouds come sneaking in. My binoculars are of little use in the semi-darkness.

Before long, our first visitor arrives, with no early warning at all. It is a barn owl which glides without a sound and alights on a branch, hardly fifteen yards away. It is only the sound of its landing and the movement of the branch that betrays its arrival. It watches intensely goggle-eyed, from its perch, for a significant length of time, slowly turning its head, for a better sighting. As suddenly as it had arrived, it floats away equally silently and returns within moments, with something dangling from its talons. I focus my lenses. The sky has lightened sufficiently to reveal a leveret, in its death throes. We watch it finish its dinner and wing away. The decapitated head of its prey remains suspended by its skin, from its perch

The hyenas and jackals can be heard, howling somewhere. Their sense of smell is keen and they might have sensed the presence of their mortal enemies. So, they keep their distance. Sounds of the night are everywhere, but poor visibility denies us a clear, sighting. A few civets can be heard quarreling on the fish-tail palm further away. But before we move away we are rewarded with the sight of a pair of porcupines with their quills raised, mating under a cashew tree. The final curtain is drawn by a fleeting glance of a little creature in black and white, with a bushy tail. The typical acrid rotten egg smell it leaves behind, confirms it is a skunk. I did hope to see a nightjar. I strain all my senses to spot one, but with no result. I have never seen a nightjar. It is past ten o'clock. "Time to turn back," says the old man.

As we begin our descent the old man narrates an incident. "Franxavier my neighbour had purchased a cow at the annual cattle fair, held following the feast of Mae dos Pobres, and was happily tending it. But within two weeks the cow disappeared, without a trace. The motherless little calf had to be hand-fed for months. Marcos as usual, was the suspect. He was a friend of Ali the butcher and it was bruited, that Marcos would steal and sell the cattle to Ali.

The narration is interrupted as Francis stumbles on a rock and falls flat on his face. He begins to bleed. We are rattled as a broken bone could be a damper to our otherwise, joyful trip. Roberto the elder son of Agostinho, runs uphill and returns with a few leaves picked from a bush nearby, crushes them in his hands and applies the extract over the wounds. Francis grimaces. To our good fortune, the wounds are not serious, the blood stops oozing and we resume our descent, this time, more cautiously as the old man continues his narration.

"Days after the disappearance, a leopard was found dead

possibly after a fight with a rival or a tiger. We bring the carcass lower down, to skin it. Along the way, we could hear the faint tinkling of a little bell, but could see no cow. I carefully skin the animal as the pelt is valuable, the less damaged the better. The teeth and the claws are also pulled out. They fetch a good price. As I turn over the carcass, the source of the tinkling is revealed. Before the remains are buried, I cut open the stomach and recover the bell. Franxavier who too is present, immediately identifies that it is the bell, he had hung around the neck of his missing cow. Marcos is acquitted, from the suspicion of cow theft!"

Tired but happy, we leave for home after our days of fun, adventure and frolic. On our way home we pester José on his 'recipe' to catch the boar. He makes us promise on our honour that we will not leak it out.

"If the general public gets into the trick, all the boars will disappear in no time. The boar ended on the kitchen table because he was stronger than all other competitors for the bananas, drove them away, consumed them all and thus fell asleep. Sometimes being stronger turns into a liability.

"All that I did was to buy some sleeping pills and push them into the bananas. The big boar devoured the bananas and landed in our stomachs. It is important that the creature recovers from its slumber before it is slaughtered. Otherwise, those who eat the meat may go to sleep. Sometimes, never to rise again." he concludes.

As we cycle back home there is news that Pobres is missing and all sorts of rumours are afloat. His only son had left the house after a disagreement with the father's way of living and was working in Dubai with his wife. For a few weeks the talk around is about what could have happened to Pobres. Somehow most people felt that he must have just run away to Bombay as has been the case in the past. He is believed to have a mistress living there involved in the distillation and sale of hooch.

We arrived home physically tired by the relentless climb up and down the hill and tanned by the exposure to the sun but mentally refreshed and enervated. Alberto is sitting in the balcao. I am taken aback to see him with a bandage below his left ear.

"I slipped on the steps and rolled down resulting in the injury. Dr. Costa Pereira is treating me. I am fine now," he explains.

I sleep well beyond waking hours. Alberto has woken up early as always and prepared breakfast, before he draws me out of bed. I go to the well and draw a pitcher of water to wash my face. I notice the gunny bags kept for drying on the parapet of the well by me, are missing. I peep into the well-not there either. At breakfast I mention to Alberto that there are rumours that the Pobres whom we had just traced has disappeared.

"Do you think he identified you and thought that his game was up and has run away?"

"How do you expect me to know that?" The response is appropriate and I remain silent.

"Do you know where the gunny bags I had kept out to dry have disappeared?"

"May be they have disappeared with Pobres. Who knows? Things and persons seem to be disappearing these days."

His cryptic retort again silences me.

Chapter 17

Ramponni

The beach is virtually empty except for a wizened old fihserman leaning against a coconut tree. I have carried my binoculars and as I scour the sky, I can see a white breasted sea eagle flying low over the waters. I keep tracking it. After about ten minutes, it swoops down and picks up a fish in its talons in a quick and swift snatch and grab. It struggles for a moment to gain height with the rather large fish weighing it down. But after a few flaps of the wings regains its equilibrium, and flies high and alights on a dead branch of casuarina, perhaps a hundred yards away.

I focus my binoculars and the struggle of the fish is distinctly visible. In no time, the sharp beak tears open the flesh and it goes down the throat, even as the fish continues to struggle. It is a catfish. I watch the bird until it has finished its lunch and flies off.

Sandpipers are dancing around in the wake of the tide. Surprisingly, there are a few brown headed seagulls bobbing up and down in the water not too far from the shore. Normally, the gulls fly away by the time summer arrives. These must be stragglers.

By and by, the old fisherman is joined by many others all similarly undressed except for a loin cloth. I count about thirty of them. Soon, they get busy loading a net on to a canoe fitted with an outrigger. All of them struggle to push the canoe into the sea and succeed after tremendous effort. Two men seated towards the rear, slowly unload the net,yard by yard into the sea as the oarsmen upfront row against the tide. The progress is tardy as the canoe moves in a westerly direction. After about three hundred yards or so, it turns south. The net is weighted at the bottom with lead while there are floats at the top. The wooden floats form a neat line on the surface of the sea and are the only indication of the net which is all underwater. One end of the net is tied by long ropes to a coconut tree on the shore. Two other canoes follow the canoe with the net to check that everything is in order and if not, to set it right.

The canoe then turns towards the shore at about another three hundred yards from the starting point. Once the canoe reaches the shore the ropes attached to the other end of the net are moored to another coconut tree. The net forms a semi-circular loop with the fish trapped within. The whole process of net laying has taken about two hours.

The tired fishermen come to shore. The fisherwomen have arrived with pots of rice gruel and pickled raw mangoes. Dried fish is roasted on an earthen pan on an open fire on the beach. The rice gruel is shared among all of them. I am the only outsider and upon being noticed I am graciously provided a helping. I thoroughly enjoy my first taste of real life in the raw.

I now comprehend that it is the old man who directs where the net should be laid and for this reason he was on the shore earlier. He has an uncanny knowledge of the sea gained over decades of experience and can, from the colour and the movements of fish in the water identify the species and gauge the best place to lay the net. His work is over as he rests in the shade of some trees. I join him. Oh, he does love to talk.

"Well young man I have my life behind me. I am merely biding my time, whatever is left of it. My bones are weary, flesh worn out. But for you everything lies ahead. Put your time to good use. Young men today are in a hurry. No respect for age. No respect at all. Sit down. I will tell you about the sea and those who try to conquer it.

My mother would tell me that six months before I was born she had first travelled by train to Margao from Majorda with my father. The railway had been laid and completed a short time earlier. And there were fears being expressed that the unborn child may be born deformed due to the movement and rattling of the bogies. I believe my mother's response was that the train is not an eclipse! Lore had it that a pregnant woman should be wary of eclipses. And she pushed on regardless, becoming the first pregnant women to travel by train or so it was said. And that makes me the first local to travel by train before birth, so said my father.

I was born on the feast day of Epiphany, hence my name Reis Magos- The Magi Kings. I am the youngest of six children who survived. Two others had died in infancy. I was pampered more than the others. I spent a lot more time with my grandmother. My mother sold fish in the village. My father helped at hauling in the nets when not drunk, which was rare. Three sisters did I have. One was married before I was born. I know her a little. She is more a mother and less a sister to me. Her second son is some months younger to me. The other two were married before I received Holy Communion. My second brother works in Bombay. And the eldest one disappeared at sea when his canoe capsized. His body was never found. Some say he fled to Africa as his wife was unbearable. So I had to bring up their children along with mine.

All the years of my life I have known nothing but the sea,

the wind and the fish. Day after day, month after month, season after season, here I am on the beach, me and my loincloth. But alcohol I have shunned. If you were my father's son, you too would. I cannot say for sure but it is said that I am nearly a hundred years old. And in these years I have seen the fires of hell. And the glories of heaven. Hell more often than heaven. And I have seen waves as high as the mountains, you see yonder. And storms that have tossed my canoe like a bit of driftwood, outrigger and all. And I have survived it all."

I have fallen in love with his lilting narrative. It is real rustic.

I begin to question him about the fishermen and their lives. He is only too glad to speak and needs no proding.

"The *rampon* is almost three quarters of a mile long but only about ten yards deep when cast in the sea. The depths of the sea contain unknown hazards, whole trees broken by the wind and carried by the tide. Rocks that emerge suddenly after a storm where there was a flat bottom. And undercurrents under a calm surface, flow unseen. The net may be pulled miles away from where it is cast. The sea can be treacherous if you do not respect it. A deeper net may get entangled and torn.

My ancestors were ignorant folks. None knew the art of knitting nets. The *Kantalli* or *Kantarri* (gill-net) was the only net they knew. Small and flimsy. Things changed when the Jesuits landed. The Jesuits had a mission house over there (he points towards the north) before they were expelled. The mission house is now owned by the Ozorio Saldanha family, powerful landlords. My daughter-in-law is their mundkar. The missionaries taught us the art of knitting these large nets and laying them at sea. Before that, all that we had were the *kantalli* with a small reach which we still use in the rains when it is too dangerous to go out in the open sea. But the big nets enable us to catch bigger fish and in greater numbers by venturing out, much beyond the shore.

Do you know how the *rampon* got its name?"

He proceeds to explain, "The priest who taught our ancestors the art of making and laying the nets was an Italian friar Fr. Batista Ramponi and the nets he made came to be known as Ramponi's nets. To this day the nets are called *ramponi* after him and the fishermen who use the nets are called *ramponkars*. My distant ancestor was named Batista in his honour and my elder brother carried the same name. It has been repeated in my family from grandfather to grandson."

As I talk, I see villagers flock to the beach – men and women, farmers, toddy-tappers, the young and old. News travels fast. A huge shoal of fish has been entrapped. Muscle power is required to haul the net ashore. All those who pull get a share of the catch.

"The task is not easy," says the old man.

"Look. Can you see the pull? Can you see the undercurrent? Look, look, how the net is drifting."

"Slacken the rope. Loosen the rope," he shouts

"The current is too strong. Let the net drift. Run along, run along," he guides.

The pull is too much. The net is only half way to the shore. Not much daylight is left. The sun is still well above the horizon. Orders are shouted to secure the ropes to the coconut trees. Tomorrow may be easier on the haul.

Small nets are in the meantime cast within the net and loads of fish are pulled to the shore. Only so much as could be sold is brought up. There are no cold storage facilities unlike in Bombay and if all the fish is hauled up, it will go waste. The rest will be harvested in the morning to be sold as the whole day will lie ahead.

I too, had helped in pulling the net. I walk home with my share of fish which is rather too much for just two of us. I keep some of the catch while I give the rest to the *Bhatkar*.

Chapter 18

Watermelon Competition

Months pass by and the competition organised by the Village Panchayat for the best water melon produced by a villager is due the following Sunday. Alberto and I proceed to the Panchayat after Mass. Farmers bring their water melons carefully tended, to the pandal set up for the purpose. A crowd of people has gathered, each person making his own guess as to who the winner will be. I see my friends Caetano, Luis and Manuel too bring their water melons for the competition and it is easy to see that they have by far the best looking water melons.

The Judges have no difficulty as the circumference of the water melons is measured and they are weighed. An hour later the Sarpanch, other members and the Secretary come out. He announces the prizes.

a) Third prize goes to Caetano Fernandes from Luis ward Calata the circumference is 103 cms weight 11.73kgs. A loud applause follows.

b) Second prize goes to Luis Fernandes of the same ward 117 cms and 13.69 kilo. Applause again.

c) And the First prize goes to Manuel Mendes, 127 cms and 15.83 kgs from the same ward. There is thunderous applause as it is announced that this year's watermelons are record breaking.

The Sarpanch stands up and makes a brief but, obligatory speech.

"I see that the competition is drawing more and more participants every year, a sign that our farmers are active. As the whole of Goa knows, the name Utorda represents quality in watermelons. The reputation has been earned over the generations by our ancestors and we have to maintain it.

"For the first time this year, Utorda has been pushed out of the winner's podium and Calata has swept the prizes. It is a welcome development as competition is the core of success. I am sure Utorda farmers will take it up a challenge and come out with greater vigour in the coming year. Calata on the other hand must try to maintain their position.

"The Calata win is a real surprise. I wonder what is the secret they have found?. I do hope they share it with the community. Maybe the secret could be applied for other agricultural practices like rice farming which could help the country reduce its dependence on import of rice. My congratulations to the winners for the surprise they have sprung on the village. You all took Utorda farmers totally off guard who I suppose must have been complacent. And let me add. Utorda has always displayed a fighting spirit. I expect them back in the ring next year to challenge the new champions".

Now it is the turn of Manuel to stand before the mike as the winner, and respond. He is extremely hesitant. He has never before appeared on a stage to speak. He is encouraged by his peers and goaded to go for it. He reluctantly steps out before the mike. His nervousness is visible. He stutters to begin with. But then, unexpectedly he gets into the groove adjusts the mike and begins his address.

"It was never my intention or that of the second and third prize winners to participate in the competition. We had planted our watermelons in normal course for home consumption and for sale in the market as in the past. But we did try something new. Still we never believed we could challenge the Utorda farmers. But as the watermelons grew, they kept on growing. We have earned more by the sale of water melons this year alone than we have earned in the last three years together. And it is not merely the watermelons that we displayed at this competition. If we were to bring more we could have swept the top hundred places. Such is the quality.

"Now do not ask me how we managed it. As farmers we have a right to keep our methods to ourselves. Has Utorda ever shared their knowhow? Why should we? Look out for next year. The best way to improve the quality is through competition. And by finding new ways to improve the crop. As we have done. Let me tell you we have produced record breaking melons this year. And if Utorda wants to beat us let them break this record.

Till then we may not even participate again. Thank you," He concludes to applause.

As we return home the friends are cocky as ever. "Tell me why did you take credit for the oversized produce when all of us know nothing about the sudden spurt in the growth of the watermelons?"

Manuel's response makes me appreciate that he is not the country bumpkin I thought he was.

"Why must we display our ignorance? Why must we let them know that it's a chance happening? Let them believe we have a secret up our sleeves. We may not produce such watermelons again. So it is better not to participate and lose. Let us maintain our record. Winners on debut and a record-breaking win. But if we do get such giant-size watermelons we can be back to improve the record. If not, we can always tell them so long as our record remains we shall not compete!"

My friends are mobbed by the villagers trying to find out what they had fed the plant to produce such record-breaking water melons. After all, none of them has had a reputation for farming. Their truthful answer is, "The usual meat waste". Nothing special."

Chapter 19

Feast of Goencho Saib

A small chapel dedicated to *Nossa Senhora das Flores* stands alone with coconut trees standing around as sentinels. It is being cleaned and spruced up. The third of December is the feast of *Goencho Saib*, time for a *ladainha* at the chapel, as in every other chapel in the land.

Winter has set in and it becomes very cold as darkness creeps in.

Devotees walk in wrapped in warm clothes. Soon the chapel overflows. A fire has been lit in a corner, beyond the chapel around which a few of the early arrivals are warming themselves.

The *ladainha* begins with the rosary being sung followed by the litany to the Sacred Heart. And a hymn to Our Lady. Alberto leads the singing. Everyone joins in. All in Latin. And it sounds so divine. Perhaps none understands the prayers. Only the rousing hymn to *Goencho Saib* is in Konkani.

Sam Francis Xaviera, vodda kunvra
Raat dis amchea mogan lastolea
Besanv ghal Saiba sharar Goyenchea
Samballun sodankal gopant tujea

Beporva korun sonvsarachi
Devachi tunven keli chakri
Ami somest magtanv mozot tuji,
Kortai mhonn milagrir, milagri.

Aiz ani sodam, amchi khatir
Vinoti kor tum Deva lagim
Jezu sarkem zaum jivit amchem,
Ami pavo-sor tuje sorxim.

It is the tradition at this chapel that after the ladainha, a village elder preaches on the significance of the day. And this task is usually discharged by the *Bhatkar*.

The *Bhatkar* rises. And begins: "I shall not speak on the life of St. Francis because this morning we have listened to it in Church. But I will touch related aspects.

"By the time Pietro Di Bernardone, a silk merchant had returned to Assisi after a business trip, to France, his wife, who was expecting her seventh child, had delivered and named him Giovanni. However, the father chose to call him Francesco (Frenchman) in view of his business success in France.

"Francesco grew up, his fame as a mystic and healer, spread all over. He was canonised, within a short time of his death as St. Francis of Assisi and is today, considered among the greatest saints of the Catholic Church. He was the first St. Francis. Most newborns came to be known as Francisco, in his honour. There are eighty-eight saints in the Catholic Church, as of now with that name, or its variation-more than any other. Great saints like St. Francis de Sales and our St. Francis Xavier whose feast we are celebrating today owe their names to him. It is now among the commonest Christian name only because the first person to be named Francesco came to be a stalwart of the Church. And parents began to name their children after him.

"We have sung all our hymns tonight in Latin except for the hymn to Goencho Saib which is the only hymn dedicated to the saint in our language. Let us see how the hymn came about.

"Raimundo Barreto, the choir master of Se Cathedral, Old Goa from the 1880's was a native of Loutolim, settled in Divar. In addition, he was entrusted with the task of collecting rent from the properties of the Cathedral, maintain accounts and disburse salaries.

"One day during the monsoons, fed by rains and roiled by stormy weather, the waters of the river Mandovi turn choppy. The choir master carrying the rent collection and the salaries cowered inside as the canoe tossed in the unruly waters. Before the canoe could touch the wharf, it capsized. As Raimundo was being carried away by the turbulent current he prayed to St. Francis Xavier to save him and vowed to compose a hymn, in his honour. At this point fishermen on the river bank saw the struggling man in the water, set out with their outrigger canoe and managed to rescue him but not his treasure.

"The choir master was immediately accused of having "organised" the canoe mishap to misappropriate the funds of the Cathedral. To save his honour Raimundo hurriedly sold his single storied mansion in Divar and paid off the dubious claim of the church. But then, he also had a genuine debt to pay. So he burnt the midnight oil, composed a hymn, set it to music and quietly practiced for weeks. TheHigh Mass on the feast day of St. Francis Xavier of the year 1893 resonated with the rendition of the new hymn before a packed congregation.

"Ever since, the hymn has become practically the anthem of the Goan Catholic community at home and abroad. Today is actually the world Konkani day as this hymn is sung the world over. It does not happen on any other day. Would the hymn have been such a success if the choir master did not have the blessings of St. Francis Xavier? Would the saint have saved the choir master had he feigned the canoe mishap?"

Chapter 20

Tujea Bapaichem Kestanv!

Late one evening we have a guest. The man struts in and from his gait it is palpable that he has made it in life. He sits down and compliments Alberto on his performance as a choir master.

"I attend service at Betalbatim and I have noticed that after you took over as choir master, the quality of the choir has improved. Everybody says so," he says.

His flattery makes me feel that he needs us for some purpose. "Are you free the coming Sunday evening?" he queries.

As a matter of fact we are usually free in the evenings. So we nod positively.

"It is my son's seventh birthday and the blessing of my newly-constructed house. I have never been home for his earlier birthdays as my work on the ship as a chief steward, has kept me away," he adds.

"So, there will be a *ladainha*, followed by dinner. I would like you to lead the singing and attend the dinner. Your charges will be duly paid."

He requests Alberto to play two songs on the piano, "In The Misty Moonlight" dedicated to his wife and the popular "Congratulations", obviously appropriate for the occasion in addition to the regular birthday song.

"Your language sounds different. Are you not a local?" I inquire.

"Not exactly, I am from Agassaim. My wife is from here. My father-in-law allotted me this plot of land where I have built my house."

On that Sunday evening at seven-thirty pm we are set for the *ladainha*. Most of the village is present. I realise that the host is an important or rich villager. The *ladainha* goes on well, as the attendees are pretty familiar with all the prayers and hymns. By eight-thirty the service is over. Time for relaxation. It is the only house electrically lighted in the locality. From the vibrating hum, it is evident that a generator is in use.

It is the first real modern house I see in the village – spacious, well designed and well furnished though a bit overdone. The wife must be having good taste, I imagine. The owner whose name I learn is Julio, is keen that I play the brand new piano as Alberto indicates that he only plays the violin and trumpet.

We begin with the hymn *God Bless This Home* followed by the birthday song for the little boy. We follow it up with *In the Misty Moonlight* dedicated to his wife. And close with *Congratulations and Celebrations*.

It is now for Julio to take the invitees around the house. Having finished that task, he displays the latest cassette player he has imported and insists that all of us listen to the song *"Iron, Lion, Zion"* by Bob Marley. He tells us there is something in the lyrics that should interest us and we must listen carefully.

The song is played and none of us notice anything special. He then replays it and urges us to pay particular attention at about one and a half minute into the song after he gives a clap. And that is when we hear the unmistakable Konkani words *"Tujea bapaichem kestanv"* being sung by Bob Marley in his song. The version goes:

I am on the rock and then I check a stock
I have to run like a fugitive to save the life I live
I'm gonna be Iron like a Lion in Zion
I'm gonna be Iron like a Lion in Zion
Iron Lion Zion

I'm on the run but I ain't got no gun
See they want to be the star
So they fighting tribal war
And they saying Iron like a Lion in Zion
Iron like a Lion in Zion,
Iron Lion Zion

I'm on the rock, (running and you running)
Tujea bapaichem kestanv
I take a stock, (running like a fugitive)
I had to run like a fugitive just to save the life I live
Tum Tho
I'm gonna be Iron like a Lion in Zion
I'm gonna be Iron like a Lion in Zion
Iron Lion Zion, Iron Lion Zion, Iron Lion Zion
Iron like a Lion in Zion, Iron like a lion in Zion
Iron Like a Lion in Zion

The song is replayed several times and everybody is now keen to know how Konkani words came to be part of a reggae song.

"I will explain the mystery, as far as possible in the words of my friend himself," volunteers Julio and proceeds to relate,

155

"I and another Goan seaman were stranded in Kingston as the ship had gone to the dry dock for repairs, having developed a serious fault. So we bide our time on shore. On the third day as we sat talking, an elderly man overheard our conversation in Konkani and surprises us with a greeting in our language. We get talking. He is overjoyed to meet us and invites us to his house, a pretty little cottage by the sea."

Julio then proceeds to recount the further story of their new friend as narrated to them in his words:

My family comes from Goa but I was brought up in Bombay. As my parents had died in my childhood, I found shelter in the kudd where I learnt to play the saxophone from the many musicians living there. I worked in a hotel and during spare time, played in a band. Finally, I managed to get a job as a deckhand on the ship with the assistance of my uncle. You know in Goa there are so many musicians, so every young man aspires to be one. But the earnings are poor. On one of my early voyages I landed in Kingston where I met this young lady with whom I instantly fell in love. I did not return back to the ship but made Jamaica my home.

As dinner was served, he put on the record player and asked us to listen to a Bob Marley song *"Iron, Lion, Zion"*. Marley sang and somewhere in the middle we are astonished to hear the words *"Tujea Bapaichem Kestanv"* from the mouth of the great Bob Marley which words you too have just heard."

Our friend provided the explanation.

My wife is a Rastafarian like Bob Marley. So I became quite familiar with him and he even encouraged me to occasionally play the saxophone for him. One day, as I jammed up with him, I offered to play my own Konkani composition "Tujea Bapaichem Kestanv" which the band enjoyed and I soon came to be named "Tujea Bapaichem Kestanv.

"I know him," jumps up Nazario from behind. "He is my cousin."

"Do not interrupt. Allow me to go on," commands Julio.

By now I am a regular part of the Bob Marley crowd. Along the way Bob Marley records a song 'Iron, Lion, Zion'. In this practice recording, he spontaneously interjects the words "Tujea Bapaichem Kestanv" on seeing me in the background. But I do not remain silent I respond "Tum tho" which is part of the chorus in my original song.

He puts the cassette again and says, listen carefully. You will hear the Konkani words *"Tum Tho"* So we listen. And indeed a few moments after *"tujea bapaichem kestanv"* one can hear the words *'Tum tho'* being softly sung.

That's me. It was part of my original song which I sung out in response to Marley.

Actually he could not pronounce the word Kestanv but he pronounced it as Kastanv which you must have noticed, says our friend.

"But why is the song not heard on radio or available at music shops? It sounds real fabulous. Should have been a hit," chimes in Fernando who sings for a local band.

"I put the same question to our friend and his response was: *Because there never was, another recording. I obtained a copy of the song on cassette which you have heard today from Bob Marley himself. Actually the recording took place very recently. May be it will be recorded again and released some day.*"

"Later our friend invited Marley for a dinner with him and we must be the only Goans to have dined with the reggae star. Have you noticed that the name 'Bob Marley' itself translates to 'shouted' in Konkani?"

Our friend made copies of the cassette one for each of us. "I will always cherish the cassette because it is a reminder to me that there is no place on earth where you will not find a Goan. From him I picked up the lyrics of *Tujea Bapaichem kestanv* and I have sung it a couple of times on the ship to the other Goan crew."

"I know him says," Nazario from behind. "It is João Paulo my cousin. He has'nt been writing of late. He married a Jamaican.

We have written to him several times to come back at least for a visit. But he has been reluctant. My father even offered to buy the tickets for the entire family. He may never come as his parents died when he was young and he has lost touch with us. It is also felt that he does not want to come because his wife is a black woman. And the reception to her in Goa may not be favourable."

Now the *Bhatkar* says, "You have to sing the song to us. It would be a privilege to listen to a song that Bob Marley enjoyed."

"I am not very proficient with the song. I may not recall the full lyrics."

"Be it so, give it a try."

"Alright, give me some time, I will sing after dinner."

The dinner was sumptuous with typical Goan dishes, some I had not tasted before. The table was laid with sorpotel, assado, stew, kingfish, xacuti, pumpkin, and what have you. It was an indicator that the host has arrived. Everyone enjoyed the meal.

After dinner, we have a practice session with Alberto on the trumpet and me on the piano. Julio sings the song *Tujea Bapaichem Kestanv* which in Konkani means "your father's quarrel" in a high baritone. It is a love ballad about a father refusing his daughter's hand in marriage to a groom because of his low caste. He finally marries another girl. And the girl he loved, elopes and marries a non-Catholic leaving her father lamenting that a low caste Catholic would be preferable to a non-Catholic. There is clapping, whistling and general applause.

Chapter 21

Evidence and Arguments

The suit has been adjourned twice as the defendants seek time to prepare and file their written statement The Judge has given 'last and final' (whatever that may mean) opportunity to the defendants to file it with a warning that for failure to comply, the suit will proceed ex-parte. Today the defendants file it. And the suit is adjourned for production of documents. Two hearings later the court is pleased to frame the issues.

Our advocate tells us that largely the suit will have to be decided on points of law as there is not much dispute on facts. He calls us to the office so that Alberto is refreshed on the facts of the case before he steps into the witness box on the next hearing. At the office our counsel reads out the plaint and explains the questions likely to be faced. He urges Alberto to be confident and not be confused.

"There is nothing to be worried about as our pleadings are factual. All you have to do is stick to the truth. I may not examine another witness to avoid delay. Besides our case is based solely on documents," the lawyer says.

During our next hearing, Alberto steps into the witness box and takes the oath. Our counsel conducts the examination in chief. Defense counsel stands up for the cross examination.

A few questions are asked which are answered neatly. And then, "Do you agree that for twenty-five years you were considered as dead?"

"Yes"

"But you are still alive. Are you not?"

"Yes"

"Do you have the death certificate of your father?"

"No."

"So it is possible your father is alive?"

" No."

"Why not?"

"Because I have the burial certificate."

"But that is only a burial certificate?"

"The church does not bury anyone unless certified dead. And the burial is more than twenty five years ago. So even if he were not dead he must be by now. How can he remain buried and alive for so long? But if you can show that my father is alive I would be extremely happy to embrace him. And withdraw the suit."

Laughter ensues in Court while the Judge smiles.

" Go on," the Judge urges as the defense counsel fumbles.

"When did you come to know of the death of your father?"

"Objections sir, unnecessary question. All details are contained at para three page two of the plaint your Honour."

Our counsel turns to page two and begins to read. The Judge stops him.

"No need," says the Judge. "Yes defense counsel, it is all there. Next question please."

"Why did it take you 25 years after the death of your father to file the suit?"

"Because I did not have the ability to know whether my

parents were dead or alive until my sight was restored as narrated in the plaint. After that, I traced the title deed, the burial certificates of my parents and engaged the lawyer as the defendant resisted my entry into the property despite my offer to compensate him for the money invested by him," Alberto replies.

A few more questions later, the cross examination is over.

"The plaintiff's evidence is closed," submits our counsel and makes an endorsement to that effect in the file.

"Now for defense evidence," orders the Judge.

"How many witnesses will you have?" He looks towards defense counsel.

"Besides the defendant one or two more."

Defense evidence commences a month later. The defendant enters the witness box and the examination in chief is recorded. The matter is adjourned for cross examination for paucity of court time.

The cross examination begins on the adjourned date.

"Who is your godfather?"

"Basilio da Costa."

"Do you know how you came to be his godchild?"

"Yes my father and Basilio were close friends and distant relatives."

"Tell me, was your father the caretaker of the property?"

"Yes he was."

"Was the status of caretaker ever terminated?"

"No."

"When did your father die?"

"About eight years ago."

"And he continued to be caretaker during his lifetime?"

"Yes he did."

"When did you become a caretaker? And who appointed you?"

"On my father's death. I just walked into my father's shoes. No one appointed me as caretaker."

"When did you come to know that Basilio had died?"

"I did not actually know of the death but there were rumours. I got full confirmation only when I met Alberto at the residence of the *Bhatkar* recently."

"Since when did you cease to be a caretaker and come to be in adverse possession?"

"It was my father who came in adverse possession on the death of Basilio. I succeeded him."

The cross examination was adjourned and completed on the next day. The defendants sought two adjournments to produce further evidence. But finally defense closed evidence without examining any more witness. The court suggests that both parties may file written arguments with relevant citations. The Court will then hear both sides orally in brief. After a couple of adjournments the process of written arguments is over and the case comes out for oral submissions.

Our lawyer stands up and begins to submit:

"The first two issues are cast on the plaintiff. And initially I shall confine my submissions on these two. I shall reserve my right to respond on issue numbers 3 and 4 after my learned friend has completed his submissions.

"Issue number 1 requires plaintiff to prove that Basilio da Costa is dead and that the Plaintiff is the son of the deceased. Towards this the Plaintiff has produced the burial certificates of late Basilio and his wife Ermina marked as Exhibit PW1/A and B respectively which gives their dates of death and burial. The baptismal certificate of the Plaintiff is at Exhibit PW1/C which identifies the deceased Basilio and Ermina as his parents. Besides, the defendant has himself admitted that the plaintiff is the son of the deceased Basilio.

"Now on to issue number 2. The proof of ownership is the deed of sale by which the property was purchased which is at ex. PW1/D. Based on the deed, the property has been inscribed in the name of late Basilio against the description of the property.

ExhbPw1/E is the Inscription Certificate. The property has been enrolled in Matriz in the name of the deceased and the Matriz Certificate is at Exhibit F. These documents conclusively prove the title of late Basilio to the property. And more importantly,the defendant cannot dispute the title since he is claiming the ownership adverse to Basilio and admits that Basilio had appointed him as caretaker of the suit property.

"These two issues have therefore to be determined in the affirmative. I crave leave of this hon'ble court to respond on the other two issues after the defense counsel has argued."

Defense counsel stands up and begins: "At the outset I shall not dispute the submissions made by the learned counsel for the plaintiff on the first two issues. But the soul of the suit lies in the two issues cast on defendants. The defence is ready to discharge the burden.

"As far as Issue number 3 ,it is not in dispute that the father of the plaintiff expired 25 years ago and had not come to Goa for the previous five years. And for these 30 years it is the late father of the defendant and the defendant himself who have been in uninterrupted possession of the property. As much is evident from reading paras 6 and 7 of the plaint. For this reason defense chose not to examine any witness to prove possession because the Plaintiff has admitted the same. Admission need not be further proved. It is also on record in the plaint itself that it is the defendant who has fenced the property, planted trees and developed it. And all this time the plaintiff whatever the reason be, has never even questioned the defendant or his father. Now that the property is ripe and ready, the plaintiff has come to pluck and enjoy the fruits. Hence your Honour, the issue ought to be decided in favour of the defendants.

"Finally issue number 4. Now it is well established that under the Limitation Act any person dispossessed of a property must seek repossession within 12 years. From the pleadings in the plaint and the statement on oath by the plaintiff, it is clear that the plaintiff's claim that the cause of action accrued only in December 1968 is fictitious. Therefore this issue has to be taken as proved. The suit ought to be dismissed." Defense counsel takes his seat.

Our counsel stands up to rebut.

"I shall be brief," he begins.

"Learned counsel for the defendant has not considered the aspect that the defendant was put in possession of the property as caretaker that is as agent of the father of the plaintiff. Defendant admits that the status of caretaker was never terminated. That being the case, where is the question of a caretaker claiming to be in adverse possession? Did he at any time renounce the role of caretaker? Nothing is on record. Interesting to note that the defendant did not even know for certain whether the father of plaintiff was dead or alive until he met the plaintiff before institution of the suit. Therefore it has to be construed that the defendant was occupying the property as agent of the Plaintiff and has no independent claim to it. It may also be considered that plaintiff has offered to compensate the defendant for the money and time invested by him.

"On the issue of limitation Sir, my submission is that time will start running from the date the Plaintiff became capable physically and mentally of asserting his legal rights. We have explained in depth the circumstances under which the Plaintiff had to live, which has not been rebutted.We have also to consider the fact that Plaintiff was working for a cause dear to all of us ie. to save the world from the Nazis. He was working for a troop carrier which was sunk, but the Plaintiff though wounded, survived. But his misery was compounded by the beggars syndicate."

The case is adjourned for Judgement.

Chapter 22

The Bhatkar Chronicles

I

The *Bhatkars* characteristically are the descendants of the original settlers who it is said came as a clan, from beyond the ghats, identified uncultivated land, divided it among themselves and developed their holdings. The later arrivals had no land and thus became beholden to the *Bhatkars*, as villages evolved.

The *Bhatkar* is not so much an individual as an institution and there are *Bhatkars* in every village. Some good, some bad, some ugly. I have noticed that this particular *Bhatkar* has empathy for the poor and the downtrodden. Thus the balcao of the *Bhatkar* is always crowded with people, morning, noon or night seeking some help or the other. I have for some time been keen to find out what goes on. This Sunday there is quite some activity so I join in.

The *Bhatkar* sits on his easy chair as those who gather around put their problem before him. Today, there is a group

of tribals from Nuvem who have a problem because another group has erected a cross to obstruct their age-old access. One young man stands out from the others. He is introduced as the Bombay-based nephew of the leader Francisco Pinto. He speaks English. The *Bhatkar* seems to know the other group also. So he suggests that they visit the disputed site to get a better view of the problem.

But the young man says that it may not help since the obstructionists are determined not to bow down. He suggests recourse to law.

"I will bear the expenses," he proclaims.

At this the *Bhatkar* looks up at him and says, "Life is not merely a matter of bearing expense. You will send the money from Bombay but who will bear the brunt of strained relationships between people who are friends neighbours and relatives?"

Bhatkar then repeats to him what Charles Dickens had said "The law is an ass", and adds "most certainly so". After a pause he puts a rider atop the ass. "The litigant feeds it. The lawyer milks it. The Judge, he rides it. And very pompously too!

He then advises them to settle the matter amicably since both groups are neighbours and they have close relations. Enmity once made may remain for generations.

"Why must you waste your hard earned money in meaningless and endless litigation?" he queries, as he offers to mediate only if they cannot settle the dispute among themselves.

The following Sunday, the *Bhatkar* on his bicycle and we on our newly-purchased cycle as also all the boys from my neighbourhood on their own cycles proceed towards Nuvem. There is a katcha road of rubble and mud up to the church of Mae dos Pobres. Beyond, there is a tarred road which leads to Margao on the south and Panjim on the north. We turn towards left and after a mile or so we take a dirt track on the right. Soon the track itself disappears and we are traversing through the deep jungle.

We have to park our cycles at a corner and then walk a few hundred yards led by one of the members of the aggrieved group. We arrive at an innocuous pathway climbing upwards. There is a group of about fifty people waiting. The people are short in stature, dark in complexion, shy and docile in appearance, except for one or two who evidently are under the influence of alcohol and are shouting incoherently.

As the *Bhatkar* walks in, silence reigns. However, as the leader of the complaining group begins to explain, the other group joins in, shouting and talking at the top of their voices. Chaos soon prevails. The *Bhatkar* urges them to quieten down but to no effect – until he threatens to walk away. Sense finally prevails.

The cause of dispute is a simple white painted Cross with a pedestal, little more than a metre and a half high. Those who have constructed the Cross allege that they have merely reconstructed the old Cross, while the others claim that the old Cross had been a few metres away and has been shifted with mal-intent. As far as I can see there is no issue as the Cross does not completely obstruct the access and a side way turn could solve the issue. That the old Cross has been shifted is also clear at the site. The property evidently belongs to the Comunidade. However, both groups are adamant and refuse to budge.

So the *Bhatkar* begins to question them. "Where do you go for Mass?"

"To the Church," is the shouted response in unison.

"What does the Church teach you?"

Silence, followed by a little boy saying Jesus is our Saviour. The *Bhatkar* pats him on the head.

"Now tell me why did Jesus come down?"

No response.

"Now I will tell you," intones the *Bhatkar*.

"Jesus came to show the way. And not to obstruct it. Do

you get me? Here your Cross is not the true Cross as it obstructs the access and creates a problem among friends. I do not think anyone of you is really Christian. Christianity is not a matter of merely attending Church but it is a matter of applying the teachings of Christ to our living. You have failed in this. But you have heads and you can think and reason. I am sure if all of you sit together you will find a solution and the right path. And be real Christians."

The *Bhatkar* ends telling them, "Call a meeting at your *maand** as you used to in earlier years, sit with your elders take your time, think clearly, and forget anger and grievances. You will find a way. The Lord will bless your efforts,"he says as we walk off adding."If you are still stuck call me"

On a Sunday morning, months later, Alberto still has a Mass to go to where the choir has to sing. As I am free and relaxed, I choose to walk home unhurriedly, after the first Mass. The fields are deserted. Crops are growing well. The weather is inviting. Butterflies hover a little above the ground. Bees buzz a little overhead. The kingfisher gives a long plaintive call, from a distance. I walk light-hearted and cheerful. Only the silk-cotton trees shorn of leaves, look sad. As the paddy field ends I climb up to the coconut grove. The ground beneath the java olive tree is littered with half open pods with beans spilling out. Roasted, the beans are edible but not particularly tasty. I pick up a few. The *Bhatkar* calls me in. He notices the beans in my hands.

"Do not eat too many of them as they are not healthy. Do you know the story of the tree?" The *Bhatkar* seems to be extremely knowledgeable about the world around him.

"I cannot understand why the tree is called java olive. It has no connections botanically with the olive or geographically with the region where the olive grows. The tree was introduced

---

* customary village meeting place

to India by the Jesuits from Java in the tropics. Botanically it is named stereculia foetida its flowers emit faecal smell when in bloom to attract flies which live on faeces."

"But I see such trees rising high before every Church. There is a mighty one at Betalbatim. Why is that?" I query.

"The tree was planted in front of all Churches in Salcete which was christianised by the Jesuits. The Jesuits noticed it was not easy to wean away those who had embraced Christianity from the earlier practice of worship of the peepal tree (*ficus religiosa*). So these new Christians were provided an alternate tree which was planted in front of a church. A special ritual was also devised and, performed at the tree on the day preceding the first novena. It is called a *maddi*. The ritual, though it was meant to be a temporary phase, is now a permanent almost meaningless part of celebrations of feasts. The Jesuits were sharp. Very sharp."

"You do not have to tell me. I am the product of a Jesuit boarding house and school," I respond.

As we talk, a group of seemingly happy people march in. One of them wishes me. I recognize him. And realise it is the same earlier group of tribal people from Nuvem. There is camaraderie between them - a complete contrast to the earlier antagonism. As *Bhatkar* sits down, all of them rush closer. I had got up to move away. I stay back. He has accurately sensed that things have been sorted out. A few of them squeeze in on the cement sofas, others stand. The natural leader of the group is a white haired patriarch who tells *Bhatkar*, "We followed your advice. The dispute is resolved."

"And what exactly did you do?"

"We sat and discussed. Those who had built the cross agreed that they had shifted the cross a little and apologized for their indiscretion."

The English speaking young man from Bombay speaks, "We then accepted the apology and since we all worship at the

Cross we decide to retain it. In fact we have beautified it and cleared the place around it. We then took spade and pickaxe and diverted the pathway. Now it is all clear."

The members present the *Bhatkar* with roasted cashew nuts and jungle berries.

The group says in unison, "We have solved the problem with the blessings of Jesus. The dispute is over."

Bhatkar is profusely thanked for his advice.

As they leave, the *Bhatkar* signals them to hold on.

"It is important to thank the Lord for giving us a solution. How can you just run away? All of us need a celebration. And what better way than a ladainha at the cross? And some food thereafter? Shall we do it the next Saturday?"

'Yes" they shout in unison.

"How many people will there be?"

"About seventy-five" is the response.

The next day, *Bhatkar* calls the village cook and requests her to prepare meat stew and *arroz refogado*[1] for about seventy-five persons with twice as many *bolinhas*.[2]

That Saturday evening, the *Bhatkar* and seven of us are on the way to Pateapur. We arrive as the devotees come in from all sides. The tribal peple are devout, familiar with the hymns and sing pretty well. Alberto at the end takes out his trumpet and plays as I sing the *The Old Rugged Cross* which none of them have previously heard. After the ladainha, we play and sing a couple of Konkani songs. A young lass comes forward and requests Alberto to play *Molbailo Dov* a song from the hit movie *Amchem Noxib* about which movie Alberto had no clue due to his circumstances. But once he took over as the choir master he was overwhelmed by the melody and soon picked it up. As he plays she begins to sing in a lovely and mellow voice.

---

1 braised rice
2 coconut cookies

At the end we are appreciated by claps and whistles. The food is served along with feni brought by Agostinho.

II

As we play football the mother of Rosario comes wailing in crying hysterically. None of us can make out what she is saying. Rosario hurries home with her. We all follow believing she is in some sort of trouble. We find her husband Bosteão was behaving irrationally and it was said he was 'possessed' by some evil spirit. He was shouting at some unseen enemy and his whole body was shaking violently. He was uncontrollable, his speech incoherent. It goes on for more than an hour. Then he collapses on the floor and falls asleep, breathing heavily. His wife says this has been happening for a few weeks. She believes he has been possessed by Maria Conçeição who had died unexpectedly a week or so before she was to deliver her first child amidst rumours that her husband had somehow killed her on suspicion of infidelity. The deaths took place generations earlier. The child too died with her. The village lived in fear as many villagers had unpleasant ghostly encounters with her. All misfortunes in the village are attributed to her.

The remedy in times of any calamity in the village is the *Bhatkar*. So Rosario his mother and we all make a beeline to *Bhatkar's* house which is in the next ward.The scene is narrated to him. She finishes the narration by saying "By morning he will be fine, but he may relapse any day."

"Do not worry, I will free him from what ails him. Bring him here on Saturday after dinner."

After two days, Rosario and his mother escort a reluctant Bosteão over to the *Bhatkar's* house. They are assisted by José, Domingos, Caetano and Alberto. A few other friends are also present. *Bhatkar* puts hessian cloth on the floor and makes Bosteão squat on it. *Bhatkar* ties a turban around his own head and begins to mumble something. Then he mutters aloud, "Yes I can see, I can see them. There is not one but two evil forces that reside in you. I shall destroy them. Now sit straight and look at me."

He then takes a few bits of charcoal in his hand and briskly circles Bosteão's head several times, at the same time loudly mumbling something. He then tells him, "You are possessed by evil spirits. I shall turn them into snakes, destroy them and free you."

The *Bhatkar*, after further mumbo-jumbo, lights the charcoal and sure enough one of the coals coils up, in the form of a snake. A speechless Bosteão stares open mouthed, at the *snake*. The process is repeated and one more *snake* emerges. The third time, there is no *snake*, and the *Bhatkar* assures him, that he had been cleared of all the evil spirits that were haunting him. All of us are astonished at the skill displayed so publicly by the *Bhatkar*. It is unbelievable.

The ashes are then wrapped, in a piece of cloth along with chillies and incense and given to Bosteão to be deposited, at a particular spot. Bosteao, recovers fully and is as sane and sober as ever. Before long, the news of *Bhatkar's* prowess as a 'ghaddi'[1] has spread all over.

A fortnight later the *Padre Vigario*[2] requests us to hold back after choral practice as he wishes to come with us to meet the *Bhatkar*. I knock on the door. The door opens and *Bhatkar* bows down and kisses the hand of the Vigario.

The Vigario enters the sitting room. We sit down.

"Well what are you up to now?" he inquires.

The *Bhatkar* apparently had foreseen the purpose of the visit and laughs as he explains that he had merely played a psychological trick on Bosteão. He had concealed, with the charcoals, a small sort of tablet, which were on sale months earlier during Ganesh festival and when lighted would rise in

1 Sorcerer
2 Parish Priest

the shape of a snake. The trick had worked and Bosteão never lost his mind again. And the *Bhatkar* never tried the trick again.

"I was afraid that you may have left the church. After all people respect you. You do not know how the uneducated behave. You must not repeat such a practice. As you know the Church has its well established ritual for exorcism. And your pranks can have a bad influence on the believers and could make them lose faith in the Holy Church and send them to a gaddi," says Padre Vigario as he takes leave.

III

A few weeks later, a fisherman from Betalbatim, comes over, complaining of the poor catch over a long period. He had consulted every 'ghaddi' and worshipped every god, but the nets return empty. He is desperate.

"Tell me first what have you done till now to placate the gods?"

"Well, first I offered a rooster. Nothing happened. The nets continued to be empty. Then upon advice I offer a goat. It cost so much. Still the nets return empty."

"To whom did you make the offering?"

"The god of the sea."

"Does the sea god not have the best of fish available for him? Will the sea god light a fire in the sea to prepare a xacuti from your rooster and goat? Why do you not use your head?"

"Now tell me who has directed you here?"

"My wife."

"Does she think I have command over your sea god?"

"No, but she thinks your advice works."

"If that be so, will you follow my advice in letter and spirit?"

"Yes *Bhatkar*."

"Have you stopped beating your wife?"

Silence

"Answer yes or no."

"No."

"Have you stopped drinking?"

"No."

"That is where the trouble lies."

"My advice will be fruitful, if and only if you follow everything I tell you. Otherwise your nets will return empty for the whole season. And you know what that means."

"Yes. I will follow everything you direct me to. But *Bhatkar*, I cannot stop drinking. Without a peg of feni it is just not possible to lay or pull a net."

"But can you not stop drinking to excess?"

"I will try."

"Now forget all your gods - sea or land. And follow what your religion teaches. You know the large property that the *Bhatkar* Erasmo Carvalho owns along the beach at Betalbatim. For the next three days put a garland of marigolds on the cross that exists in the property, and pray a Rosary before it with your wife and family. The garland must be made lovingly by your wife. If you abuse or beat her, the Holy Cross will know it from the garlands. And do not drink to excess. If not, your prayers will not be effective. It is up to you. On the fourth day confess you sins, attend Mass, say a final prayer before the cross with all the workers of your rampon and then lay the rampon. You will harvest a bumper harvest of the best fish."

Days later, the fisherman returns, with a basket full of choice assorted fish and thanks the *Bhatkar*. He has been having a bumper harvest.

"Have you started beating your wife?" inquires the *Bhatkar*

"No *Bhatkar*, I do not beat or abuse her."

"Good, the moment you do that your blessings will go. Do you understand?"intones the *Bhatkar* as the fisherman departs

"You are very religious," I tell *Bhatkar*.

"No, not at all. Jesus of Nazarene did not found a religion. He was a teacher. Two exemplary things were taught by Jesus

(a) separation of Church and State (b) Equality of all men. "But you have got him to pray....."

Bhatkar interrupts. "My advice has not much to do with being religious or not. It is practical advice. This man as could be seen has a belief in some divine power to help him. And I channelised that power. I believe that everyman must be true to the faith he follows. He is a Christian and I showed him the path laid for a Christian. You must remember that God is the strength of the needy

"Do you believe that God exists?"

This question arises because there is no empirical way of establishing whether God exists or not. But the answer may not be relevant at all. God will continue to exist or not exist irrespective of your or my belief or non-belief in him. There need not be a God for one to believe in Him. Is it not?

"Would you give the same advice to a Hindu?"

"Not the same. But modified, to meet the situation and his needs. So many Hindus come here. That Suresh who is frequently here or that Shashikant."

"Would the Hindu pray at the cross?"

"Why should he? On the contrary I would advise him to go to a Hindu place of worship and perform his religious obligations. I believe everyone must perform duties enjoined on him by the faith he practices. Our failure to do so is the principal cause of our backwardness.

After all there is no way to determine one religion is right or the other is wrong. For everyone his own religion is always right. For all that matters, all religions may be completely off tangent. I believe the latter is a distinct possibility," he adds.

"How does beating or not beating the wife affect fish catch?" I ask.

"That has no bearing at all. But the fisherman's wife is the daughter of our *mundkar** and she frequently runs back to her parental house because of the beatings he gives her. He comes back, takes her home and keeps repeating his obnoxious conduct. So I took advantage of the situation to provide some protection to her by linking the lack of fish catch to God's displeasure with his treatment of his wife. Hopefully it will last."

"How did you know that fish would arrive after three days?" I queried.

"Fish always come to their natural feeding grounds, depending on the weather. Unfavourable conditions may sometimes delay the arrival. It is the same for us, if the first train is delayed we wait till it arrives; If it is cancelled we go by the second. If the fish were not to arrive after three days, I would simply tell him that God is not impressed as he did not pray sincerely and he must repeat the process. The second time, the prayers would be more fervent and rigorous!" replies *bhatkar*.

---

* Caretaker

Chapter 23

The Countermanding

Bhatkar seems to be keenly following the Assembly election process which has commenced. He is opposed to the ruling party. One early morning he calls me and gives me a copy of the newspaper West Coast Express and says, "Read here."

I take the paper and begin to read the banner headline, *"Elections to Two Constituencies Countermanded" It reads: Margao Dec17: The Returning Officer to the Assembly Constituencies of Raia and Colva has in an order passed late in the evening countermanded the elections to the two constituencies. Consequently elections will be held to only 28 of the 30 Assembly seats. The elections to these two seats will be held later. It was a day of dramatic developments.*

It may be recalled that nomination process for the Assembly elections had closed days ago. Scores of candidates have filed nominations. The day following the closure of nominations was fixed for scrutiny when objections may be raised against any nomination. If the objections are upheld, nomination papers are liable to be rejected. The party in power as usual looks invincible in the constituencies of Salcete Taluka. The sitting MLAs come for the scrutiny and a very powerful and confident minister stands up and states:

"I do not object to any nomination. I believe the decision must be left to the voters and any irregularity in the nomination papers must not be taken seriously."

Nevertheless, the scrutiny goes on as the Returning Officer is duty bound to verify and admit or reject the nomination papers with or without objections.

The ruling party leadership is of course unaware of what is going on, behind the scenes. A group of young activists hostile to the ruling party but with the tacit support of a rival faction within that party are determined to teach senior leaders of the party a lesson because they take the voters for granted despite their unstinted loyalty. The plan is to delay the elections in two or three constituencies till after the Assembly is constituted and a new government comes to power. Chances of defeating these leaders are higher if the voting is somehow delayed till after the general elections. The one way, elections can be delayed is through death of a candidate as elections to the affected constituency get countermanded.

A week after the scrutiny, a candidate Pedro Dias is reported dead. He had filed nominations for the seats of Raia and Colva. All sorts of rumours begin to circulate. It finally comes to light that the family of a man on his death bed was sufficiently compensated to make him file his nomination papers. But he was too sick to appear before the Returning Officer and someone else impersonated him. The person as it happens is illiterate and had put his thumbprint on the nomination papers.

The case is vehemently argued before the Returning Officer by a team of bright young lawyers who cited law and case law to the effect that upon the death of a candidate, whose candidature has not been rejected at scrutiny, elections necessarily have to be countermanded. It was their case that even if there was impersonation for the purpose of the elections, it had to be highlighted at scrutiny and the nomination papers rejected. If not, and the candidate under whose name nomination papers have been filed is the actual candidate and on his death, elections have to be countermanded.

The advocate representing the ruling party candidate could not counter the arguments at all. Their argument that the dead man had not appeared before the returning officer carries no weight as it was open to the party to point it out at the time of scrutiny and get the nomination rejected. Such is the finding of the Returning Officer. The minister full of airs who had so pompously submitted before the Returning Officer that he does not object to any nomination was now chastened as the Returning Officer made the official announcement of countermanding the elections.

The ruling party finds itself being made to look like novices by a group of street smart activists including a doctor and a couple of lawyers. An offence has been registered and investigations begin. The first step for the police is to confirm the thumb impression on the nomination papers is not that of the deceased who has since been buried. An order has been obtained from the Sub Divisional Magistrate to exhume the body.

Chapter 24

The Exhumation

Alberto and I are sitting with the *Padre Vigario* to finalise the programme for the novenas preceding the Church feast. As we discuss, we can hear heavy footfalls on the rickety wooden steps leading up to the first floor of the residence of the priest. Soon, three policemen appear and sit down by our side.

The Police Inspector in charge, explains to the *Padre Vigario* that they need to exhume the body of late Pedro Dias. *Padre Vigario* looks aghast and says that as per church law, once a person is buried, the bones are to be exhumed only after three years. But, the policeman points out that he has an order from the Magistrate.

The priest tells him, "I only take orders from above. It is our belief that the dead will be raised when Jesus comes again on the day of Judgement. I have no powers to raise a man lawfully buried. Only Jesus can do that."

The answer stuns the policeman, who murmurs, "But I have orders."

"If you have orders, you may follow them. Have I stopped you?"

"But how can I? I do not know where the grave is."

"Neither do I," says the *Padre Vigario*.

"It is only the *pedo* who keeps track of the burials. He lives by the side of the church; you may find him now, if he is sober."

The priest deputes me to show them the residence of the *pedo*, while he continues to finalise the details of the programme for the feast with Alberto.

We descend the stairway which continues to complain. We turn around and go by the side of the church, where the *pedo* lives. The door is open and the wife of the *pedo* is squatting on the floor, cleaning some rice. She jumps up on seeing the police and cries: "What has Francis done now? Please do not arrest my husband he is a good man, although he drinks and sometimes behaves in a disorderly manner. He means no harm."

"Do not worry," says the PSI. "I have not come to arrest him. I merely need his assistance that may help me in an arrest."

"But he is not here."

"Where is he likely to be?"

"Check the tavern, over there," she points out.

We walk towards a little tavern just in time to see Francis walking back to the house inebriated as usual. He wishes me but the presence of policemen unnerves him.

"I have done nothing," he cries.

"Certainly you have done nothing," says the Police Officer to calm him. "I only need your help to catch someone who has done something wrong."

The police officer explains to him that he is required to exhume the grave of Pedro Dias early in the morning before sunrise. Francis looks askance.

"I cannot do so. I cannot reopen a grave without the express orders from the *Padre Vigario*, besides no grave is ever opened up unless three years have elapsed from the burial. It does not do good to disturb the dead. It is a bad omen. I know of cases where the disturbed dead, haunt those responsible, for the rest of their lives. I will not touch the grave. You too, better be careful."

The Police Officer is visibly disturbed. But he has to do his duty. He discusses the matter with his subordinates. It is agreed that they will bring in the two men earlier arrested and in police custody for some offence, to do the work. So the police officer tells the *pedo*.

"Will you please show us the grave where Pedro is buried?"

"Yes I can do that."

"There is a cross at the head of every grave carrying the name of the person inside it. It is easy to locate a grave".

"All right," says the police officer.

"We shall come in the morning and wake you up. Please do not give any excuse. You have experience of what happens to those who disobey the police."

The police go their way. After the police jeep roars away and they are beyond hearing distance the *pedo* tells me.

"I know what they are after. They do not know that a *pedo* can be more dangerous than a police officer. I will teach them. Experience, I certainly have. But now it's payback time. And I will do so with interest. Let them come tomorrow."

My curiosity is greatly aroused and I am determined to witness the happenings. I contact José and Antonio who readily agree to join the predawn adventure. Before dawn breaks, I can hear the signature whistle used by us to gather together. I am ready within minutes. It is pitch dark and José has a torch which seems to cast more shadow than light. Both carry bamboo bits about a yard long. We soon traverse the coconut grove and descend into the paddy fields which open to the sky. The sky glitters with stars too far away to to mitigate the darkness. José and Antonio move ahead noisily in single file as that is all that the narrow ridge on which we walk, permits.

Either side is overgrown with weeds and thorny bushes. They swish the sticks from side and to side and disturb the

overgrowth ahead, seemingly determined to show their presence.

"Why are you all so noisy?" I question them

"Because all these fields are hunting ground for all sorts of nocturnal creatures. Among them are Cobras, Russel's vipers and Kraits. If anyone of them bites, you will end up where we are presently heading. And remain there permanently."

"If so why alert them to our presence? Will it not be appropriate to move silently?"

They both laugh out loudly. "Do you think these creatures are hiding here waiting to bite you? Essentially they are here either looking for food or mates. And they are as afraid of us as we are of them," retorts José.

"You see if you step on any of them you may be bitten back in self-defense. They do not have the human propensity for vengeance," he volunteers.

"We walk noisily to alert these creatures of our presence so that both keep a safe distance."

As we talk, we soon reach our target. Now we slow down and take a vantage position and crouch by the cemetery wall. And wait. And wait. We can see a police jeep parked outside with a few persons inside it.

The police arrive somewhat late in the cemetery with the *pedo* in tow. They berate the *pedo* for causing delay. The police are accompanied by two persons who I conclude are the two detainees, clearly brought against their will to perform the unpleasant task. Both carry spades. The *pedo* walks ahead. Others follow. One policeman carries a petromax, another one a torch. The *pedo* points to the grave. After sometime he tells the police he has to ring the Angelus bell and hurries away. From my place I cannot read the name on the cross. Accompanying them is a doctor in a a white coat wearing gloves and carrying forceps. The unwilling grave diggers look pathetic as they get on with the unholy task. Spade by spade the mud covering the grave is scooped up. The burial is recent. The mud is loose. The task is not difficult.

Finally the diggers hit wood. And hit a problem too. The lid of the coffin is three feet below the ground. The grave is a little larger than the coffin. The fit in the grave is snug. There is no scope to enter the grave to lift the coffin. The coffin needs to be lifted the way it was lowered with ropes and four men to hold. But there is no rope in sight. The policemen go looking for the *pedo* again. After quite a search as we can see,he is found and he directs them to a corner of the cemetery. The ropes are traced. He refuses to help and walks away, casually.

The rope is passed through the handles. There is a mighty heave. The coffin lifts. The rope tears. The coffin is back in the grave. Another rope is obtained from the corner. And a second heave. The coffin lifts upwards to the surface. And it falls back again. The handles have come unstuck. The cops pant and curse. The unfortunate detainees have now to dig the grave and enlarge the pit at the head and feet. Fifteen minutes later the cops descend into the space created and lift up the coffin. As the coffin is opened the stink of decaying flesh fills the air. The doctor tries to carry out his task but I can hear him say he is helpless to get a thumbprint as the flesh has disintegrated and melted. Nevertheless he takes prints, whatever way he can, on police insistence. The coffin is hurriedly closed and lowered. The police look around for the detainees to refill the grave. No one is around. The two have fled through the darkness. The policemen have to do the work of the *pedo*. The Angelus bell rings, as the police walk out of the cemetery.

Dawn is creeping in and the police are visibly relieved. As they walk to the jeep, one of the policemen starts to vomit and retch. The contagion spreads as others join in, except the forensic doctor. He is accustomed to the stench of decomposing corpses. The *pedo* who was drawing water from the well rushes in with an earthen pitcher. The grateful policemen take it wash their faces and gargle their mouths. After about five minutes normalcy returns. As the police thank him, he says to the police inspector, "Did I not tell you that it is a bad omen to disturb a man from his grave? See, his curse has started working!"

The driver switches on the engine and revs it up. The *pedo* continues to talk. I can see the police officer respond. But we hear nothing as the noise of the engine drowns it. The doctor takes the front seat while the others jump into the rear. The jeep roars off, away from the stink.

As it is day break, I offer breakfast to my friends. We walk towards the well. The *pedo* is not present. We draw a pitcher of water and refresh ourselves. And then we are at Anjona a little teashop by the side of the church.

As we walk home we see the *pedo* come out of the cemetery. He beckons us. And breaks into peals of laughter as he comes towards us.

"Everything went better than planned. First time the rope broke and the coffin fell back. I had made a cut in the rope and weakened it. Then it fell back again as the handles broke. I had no role there. It was a poor man's coffin. And therefore cheap. After the coffin was opened and all attention diverted, my replacement gravediggers slowly walked in the darkness and jumped out. And landed almost into my lap. You should have seen them run. And you should have seen the policemen do the work of the *pedo*. Nothing was ever more satisfying!

'But after all they are human. They began to vomit. I took pity on them and gave them water from the well. And I reminded them of the curse of the disturbed dead which I had mentioned yesterday," he adds as he looks towards me.

'By the way where are the gravediggers you had with you?" I ask.

"The Officer said that they let them go."

"You see they will not go after those two. They must have been arrested for some minor offence. The police will have to explain what those two were doing in the cemetery so early in the morning, if they are shown as escapees from lawful custody. So those two are fortunate.

'They may have also escaped the charge sheet! I suppose the work of digging the graves which they were compelled to do against their will is sufficient punishment for whatever offence they may have committed."

Chapter 25

T*h*e Actors

The Election Commission has announced fresh dates to fill up the seats left vacant due to the countermanding. Campaigning is in full swing.

Election meetings go late, sometimes past midnight as the candidates are busy with other meetings.The voters are attracted and kept entertained by organising a *teatro*, which breaks for interval when the candidate and other speakers arrive.

This particular meeting had the group of Rodsons performing a very well known *teatro* and the crowd was massive perhaps more for the *teatro* and less for the meeting. Among the actors are my friends Domingos and Francis. They find themselves short of an actor to play the role of a constable as the regular actor has taken ill at the last moment.

"It is a minor role. You have merely to dress in police uniform and follow the commands of the officer which role is played by me. Why don't you step in?" urges Domingos.

I have acted in school plays for years. Why not accept the offer is my question to myself. I agree to take the role. Alberto is not aware of my role.

I learn that Bhatkar is due to address the meeting. And that is an additional incentive for Alberto to attend. The tiatro is reaching its high point when the candidate arrives with his supporters, and the curtain comes down for the interval. As the stage gets set for the meeting, a group of goons owing allegiance to his opponent, who is the sitting MLA, and against whom the countermanding is directed, come charging in with batons threatening to attack. The police force, as if on cue has made itself scarce and there is a real danger of violence. As the candidate and his entourage cower in silence, a police inspector and couple of policemen in uniform suddenly emerge almost from thin air.

The constables are carrying handcuffs and the police officer shouts orders to arrest the trouble makers. The goons are caught unawares by the unexpected police presence and hastily run away with the police making a valiant effort to catch them. The meeting starts and gets over quickly as it is getting late.

I can see Alberto sitting in about the fifth row from the stage. He was keen to hear the Bhatkar's address which turned out to be short and humorous. I had come both for the meeting and for my first *teatro* which was a real entertainer and the crowd enjoyed every moment with claps and whistles. It also happens to be the first and last *teatro* in which I act.

After the meeting is over, the *teatro* resumes post interval when the villain is hiding in a jungle. The police come looking for him. As he tries to run away, Francis as constable, pounces on him and I as the other constable assist him as the villain kicks and struggles to get away. The inspector puts him in handcuffs despite which the struggle continues. So we have to tie him, with ropes and carry him away. My role is now over and I change to my regular clothes and sit in the audience.

The next day Bhatkar mentions how frightened he was when the goons charged.

"The timely police intervention saved us," says a still shaken Bhatkar.

"But do you know who the policemen were?"

"How do you expect me to know the police?"

"Well they were your neighbourhood friends Domingos Francis and I."

"Have you all joined the police force?"

"They are acting as policemen in the *teatro*. I was a last minute replacement for a sick actor."

"Do you mean the presence of mind of you guys saved the day for us?"

"Very much so."

"Actually it was an unplanned and impromptu decision by Domingos when he saw that you and the others were in danger. He roped in both of us and we rushed out. The goons could not make out the difference and ran away on seeing the men in uniform and the revolver with the inspector and the handcuffs with us."

"Well I knew they were stage actors. But I did not know they were so good. And off stage too. None of us also could make out the difference either. Your quick thinking saved us then," concludes the Bhatkar.

Days later it is learnt that the actual Police Inspector was punished by his superiors and transferred to the Reserve Police for *dereliction of duty*. He was brought back after the truth was realised. As the police had actually *kept away* there was no dereliction of duty!

Chapter 26

The Forensic Report

A fortnight later, I meet Francis the *pedo* returning from the tavern. And he narrates,

"I have taught them such a lesson that they never will catch the culprit for the countermanding. And they never will know what exactly has hit them. I was actually waiting for an opportunity to get at the police, particularly the same police officer. And the opportunity walked in. Uninvited. A year back when I was arrested for drunken behaviour, he beat me up mercilessly. I am a Goan. Don't I have a right to drink? Today, I have got my revenge. I will not tell you now, but only after the Month's Mind for the deceased Pedro. By that time it will be too late for the police to do anything."

A few weeks later, reports in the press indicate that the police could not get a proper thumbprint of the exhumed body as it had decomposed much more than it ought to, for some inexplicable reason. The forensic laboratory in Hyderabad has stated so, in its report. The police thus cannot establish whether the thumb print on the nomination papers is that of the deceased or not.

I meet Francis again after Sunday Mass. He walks cockily towards me, smiling broadly. He has a wonderful set of teeth.

"Have you read the newspapers? I had told you so. How could they ever get proper fingerprints? You see all I had to do was merely exchange the Cross from one grave to the other. The body they exhumed was actually of Cosme who had died a month previously and his body had decomposed. The Month's Mind Mass was held two days earlier. I replaced the Cross on the grave of Cosme with the Cross of Pedro and the police unaware, exhumed Cosme's body and obviously could not get a proper fingerprint. And even if they were to get fingerprints they would not match. I have over these four decades as a *pedo*, buried bodies in different stages of decomposition. And I must tell you they all look the same. No way can one distinguish the decaying corpse of Pedro from that of Cosme even if you were close friends. The Cross is the only identification mark.

"You remember on the day of the exhumation I met you and your friends as I came out of the cemetery. After the police had left I went in, replaced the crosses in their rightful place and made up the grave to perfection as I do with all burials. After all a member of Cosme's family could get suspicious if the grave was found disturbed. And then I disturbed the grave of Pedro as if it had been opened and hurriedly closed. One has to consider all angles. Sure enough the family of Pedro came later in the day to inspect the aftermath. I obliged them by restoring the grave. To profuse and sincere thanks and a tip.

'Such a lesson has never been taught to the police before. And the officer will not forget it in a hurry. Remember you must never threaten a *pedo*! Never! The police investigation is dead. And buried by the same *pedo*!"

'You better remain silent the police may trouble you,' I suggest.

"No way," says he as he goes on, "The police officer will stand exposed for his incompetence if he dares touch me. I bet the police will never admit the wrong grave was exhumed. And the authorities and the Court will always believe the police. And not the damned *pedo*. Anyway who believes a *pedo*? He is a lowly creature! And a drunkard. Is he not? Suits me, you see."

The inexplicable reason is now explicable; I say to myself and wonder at the simple ingenuity and clear logic of the *lowly pedo* which has thrown an entire investigation off track. Sometimes an illiterate shows greater ingenuity than a seasoned investigator.

Chapter 27

Birdshoot

The monsoons over, the lakes are bunded, the water impounded. A fresh crop of watermelons is growing. As the temperatures in the northern latitudes cool towards freezing, flocks of birds fly down South. Goa is a prominent spot in the itinerary of the feathered tourists. Guns are taken out, polished and checked ready to boom at the first sighting.

Bhatkar cleans his muzzle loader. And off we go. José and Caetano join us. The first victim is a purple heron standing alone with its long neck pointing towards the sky in the paddy fields. The lake is still some distance away. The gun is aimed and fired. The heron is hit and can't take off. José picks it up.

"When it is birds always use a muzzle loader you can bring down several birds with one shot." That is Bhatkar's logic in support of the muzzle loader.

We continue our march, slowing down as we reach the margin. Bhatkar takes cover behind a bamboo grove. We remain unobtrusive. Coots, cormorants and ducks abound, spread all over. Bhatkar waits for long for no apparent reason. After nearly three quarters of an hour he takes careful aim and pulls the trigger. As the gun booms, birds fly away in fright. Two drop from the flight in the fields. Three flutter in the lake. José wades in the water and picks them up. I pick up the two from the murky fields.

"Well I delayed shooting so that the birds would slowly converge, usually the same species move together. I aimed at the mallards which are more fleshy and tastier. The common teal is no good. You get only one chance and you must be careful to use it to full benefit. If you miss you are lost. Because once disturbed by the noise of the gun the birds do not return for long."

The ruins of what was certainly a large mansion greet us as we take a detour and bypass the regular trail hoping to come across other game. The house had enormous columns and from the height of the standing walls it must have been a storied structure.

José ventures, "These people have paid for their sins."

Bhatkar keeps quiet, which is quite unlike him. The ruins are overgrown with jatropha and other trees. As we proceed we see the ruins of two small mud houses. Bhatkar turns to José and pointing towards these ruins, queries, "Whose sins have these people paid for? The poor take vicarious pleasure in the ruins of the richman's house. One must not believe these stories".

"Many of the ruins are signs of success whether it is the house of the rich or poor. Not of failures. Our people have historically moved abroad for employment. And, like most immigrants worldwide, have been successful through honest hard work. Some extraordinarily so. And for these, the riches earned abroad are far greater, hence their inheritance pales into insignificance. It is only the rare failures who come back. The successful have moved to Europe, USA, Australia, Canada or elsewhere".

"Take the case of Martinho and his wife who come to see me with a complaint, 'The Hindu is not vacating'

"They were mundkars of a house in Seraulim but had, on humanitarian grounds, allowed a homeless Hindu family to live in their house on a temporary basis as they were living in Bombay. They had retired and wanted to come back to their house. But the occupants claimed to be mundkars under the changed law and refused to vacate."

"I learn that the husband has been working in Bombay for more than 40 years and the family is living in quarters rented out from a Parsi in Dhobitalao. So, I ask them, whether they had quit the premises. The response was prompt and vehement.

"Why should we? We have been living there for so long and the builder has now made an offer and we are negotiating for more."

"I ask them, Do you know what the Parsi is saying?

The response was in the negative.

The Christian is not vacating is what the Parsi is saying, I tell them. I never saw them again. You see if these people were very successful in Bombay they would not come back to evict the homeless Hindu family."

Chapter 28

Drying Pond

A few years later, the local pond nearly dries up and Roque notices the handle-bar of a cycle sticking out of the drying muck. He tries to pull it out but is unable to do so, as it has a whole cycle attached to it, which is sunk deep under. All of us gather and dig into the mud and retrieve the cycle covered in muck. It is a Raleigh. We push it to the other and deeper end of the pond which holds water till the monsoons break. Coconut husks are used to brush it clean. It is still in good shape though rusty in places with the tyres heavily leached. The aluminium licence tag indicates that the cycle is registered at the Nuvem Panchayat under number sixty-seven. The police are informed.

Later, on checking the Panchayat records, it is realised that the cycle had belonged to Pobres. The mystery of the disappearance of Pobres is revived after a few years. It is now theorised that he committed suicide by putting a heavy stone around his neck, and jumping into the pound or was murdered, weighted and

dumped in to the pound and for which reason his body never surfaced. Now, to check this theory, the pond has to be desilted. The police have neither the desire nor the finances to dig to the bottom of the pond. Besides, it is better for the police to let the issue lie because if the body is found a case will have to be registered and investigated.

But the wife of the deceased is determined to go to any depth to find out what happened to her husband and go to the bottom of the pond and the mystery. Towards this end, she hires labourers from Nuvem who for several days excavate the silt until there are a few conical hillocks of silt on the sides of the pond.Scores of curious people gathered on the banks of the pond everyday with each one having an opinion of where the body could be. A slight sound of the spade hitting something other than mud immediately attracted attention. By the end of the week, workers have dug nearly one and half metres deep under. The leader of the work men refuses to dig further as he says the bottom of the pond has been reached. As evidence, he points out how the soil at bottom is brownish red as compared to the dark grey silt that has been unearthed. The natural bottom of the pond is visible. No skeleton is found. The villagers gleefully share the silt in their own paddy fields and are glad that Pobres dead or alive has de-silted the pond for them.

As we have dinner, I mention to Alberto that the digging is over and no body was found.

"Not exactly, but nearly everybody else did".

"The diggers dug well; but did not dig the wells!"

I am perplexed. "What then do you think has become of Pobres?" I question

"The prize winning watermelons! Do watermelons automatically grow outsized and prizewinning? For three months the vines thrived on fertiliser they had never before got and never after will. And I watched the watermelons grow big and round. I was not aware of the competition though."

"That does not answer my question. Where did Pobres go?" I question

" Does it not appear he went into the watermelons?" he mumbles and looks at me

I am puzzled even more to hear that; after   deep thought I inquire

"Did he go in the gunny bags as you seemed to have hinted earlier?" I am tentative.

"You are on the right track"

"And so, you killed him?" is my pointed question.

"Do you think I am capable of killing anyone? "

"But from what you have said it appears the man is dead" I retorted.

"Yes, he is. But does that mean that I have killed him? Does it follow that the *pedo* who carries out burials has killed the corpse in the coffin? Sometimes people invite their own deaths. And no one is to be blamed."

"I am confused. Will you be more categorical?"

"Let me explain," says Alberto. "You see we left for the hills with your friends and you will recall that I returned back, the same evening. I was feeling out of place among you young people. On my way back I noticed Pobres was cycling ahead and I speeded up and caught up with him. I soon confirmed my suspicions. I was pretty sure it was him. He had no inkling who I was. Why should he remember me? He must have played the trick on scores of others. Besides, now I look totally different.

"As we talked I dropped the hint that I had a property for sale. I planned to migrate to Canada to be with my children, I lied. He fell for it and gave me the salesman's talk dropping several names of satisfied customers who have purchased plots or houses through him. He offered to come over immediately to see the property. He followed me home. It was past seven but there was light enough. I showed him our house. As mosquitoes were buzzing around I called him in and offered him a drink. His demand was for three percent commission on the sale proceeds to which I readily agreed. I offered him a bonus of two percent if he could complete the deal within three months. Mighty glad he was.

"As we got more informal, I mentioned to him that he looks and his voice sounds very familiar and enquired whether he was in Bombay. In fact, he says he spent most of his life in Bombay.

"You look so much like Inacio D'Melo whom I knew in Bombay. As I say these words, I focus on his face which visibly changes colour. I knew I was on the right path."

"Who is Inacio?" he queried.

"Inacio, was an agent of a beggar's syndicate who would visit hospitals, befriend poor and abandoned patients, gain their confidence and sell them to the syndicate. The police are looking out for him. And so am I."

"I am not him," he says in anger.

"You are very much him and you sold me to the syndicate."

"You are defaming me with false and malicious allegations. The whole of Salcete knows me and respects me. I do not know what you are talking," was his defensive response.

"Do you remember you went to the Majorda Club at Jer Mahal claiming to be the nephew of Basilio D Costa? Do you remember that you offered to pay the fees dues, if any to take away his trunk? Are you not the one? Were you not told to bring a court order? Do you want witnesses who knew you when you were living at a club in Girgaum? How will you run away?" I grill him.

"By tomorrow, the police will be in the know. And I know other people who have lodged other complaints against you.I will see that you go to jail and remain there.I realise you were Inacio D'Melo in Bombay and you are Pobres D'Souza in Goa.

"At this, he turned red and infuriated. His game was up. He stood up and pounced on me with a knife which he had apparently carried with him. As I feinted to one side I got the knife cut below the ear. But I had half anticipated his move. He lost his balance when I stepped aside as he lounged at me. He stumbled and struggled. I picked up a chair and hit him. Fortunately for me it was a heavy teak wood chair. I hit him with all force goaded by the anger boiling inside me for the years of suffering he had inflicted upon me. He was much bigger than me and I would have had no chance against him in a one to one contest. I hit him again as he tried to rise and kicked my arm. And again and again. And I hit very hard. He fell down, moaned for some time and then fell silent. I tried to revive him but to no avail. He was dead within a few minutes. Blood spilled on the floor. His head was smashed.

"I had the option of reporting to the police but I realised that no one would believe me and I may have to spend the rest of my life in jail. My miraculously gained freedom could be lost. After all, I have spent twenty years in jail. I mean being blind is worse than being in jail, particularly, if you are young hale and hearty and when you could see normally before the blindness was forced upon you.

I struggled to find a solution. In a flash I remembered what *Bhatkar* had said about what happens in Court. "Never go to a court. Never. It is a waste of time and money. *What we have are courts of law not courts of justice. So rarely will you get justice in a court. You may get a judgement though.* You know we had to file a suit against Damiao as a last resort. Another Court proceeding was out of the question.

And I cannot forget what Bhatkar had finally said. *A successful lawyer is he, who first confuses himself, then he seeks to confuse opposing counsel and finally he seeks to confuse the Judge. If he succeeds it is called justice.* I did not want to be caught in such confusion. So the police and Court were ruled out."

"And I sit and ruminate on the next course of action. I know that if no corpse is found there is no murder. How do I get rid of the corpse? A gust of wind brings in the stinking smell of rotting offal from the water melon wells. And I say to myself even God is with me. He has provided the solution. I have to follow it."

"Quickly, I set about the macabre task and drag the body into the kitchen and butcher it. In fact, I was in such frenzy that I did not know what I was doing. There was mincemeat where there was Inacio half an hour earlier. The kitchen was a bloodied mess. Fortunately you had brought those gunny bags which came in handy. I packed three bags and wrapped the bags in the canvas cloth that was lying in the storeroom, to prevent blood dripping along the way. It was midnight, as I straddle the bags on the cross bar of his cycle and push the cycle through the darkness into the fields. It was tiring work pushing the cycle carrying a load of some eighty kilos or more. I dumped a gunny bag one each into the water holes. On my return I deflated the tyres, for fear the cycle may float and discarded the cycle into the murky pond."

"I was home, in a hurry. I spent considerable time washing the floor. Next morning, I got up at sunrise and again clean up the house as also the compound where blood had dripped. Later I retraced the path the cycle had taken in the night. Blood did ooze out along the path. I carefully wiped out all traces with my feet. I burned the canvass to ashes. I proceeded to the house of Dr. Costa Pereira who sutured the cut. I am fortunate that I suffered no injuries that would have disabled me from the gruesome task I had to perform. No evidence of the previous night's happenings is left. You recall that you were surprised that the kitchen and dining room were painted by the time you had returned. And I had told you I had done it because I had time on hand. Now you know why the walls had to be painted. Tell me, why did you bring those gunny bags?"

Still stunned, I respond, "Oh those bags, I had been to the local shop where these bags had been emptied of their contents of rice, sugar, wheat, etc by the shop keeper and stacked outside for sale. I felt they may be useful as doormats particularly during the monsoons, so I purchased a few. Now I realise what you had meant when you had quipped that the gunny bags may have gone with Pobres. Only instead of doormats they turned out to be funeral shrouds!"

Alberto continues. "I believe that it was destined to end this way. Sometimes the forces above choose to dispense justice on earth. I was the vehicle of justice. May be by the act, other injustices have been averted. He died at my hands. And in my house. But I did not murder him. Murder has a different connotation. Of course if I were caught it would be murder. Because neither the public nor the police know the distinction. Neither would I be able to prove it. And there was a mere split moment to act. If it was not him it would be me. And I had not survived to die at the hands of the very man who had sold me to the syndicate. And ruined me. That would be an ultimate act of injustice. So I became the dispenser of justice."

"Have you noticed that the local boys have not been able to

match the prize winning watermelons produced by them when they swept the prizes? I am certain by now you know how such wonderful and prize winning water melons were produced at that time."

"Do you remember that the Sarpanch had advised the winners to share the winning secret with the farmers? Do you want to share it?" I needle him in jest.

One case is over without registration of any offence. But our property suit is now drawing to a close after a surprisingly short trial. Our lawyer says it is because we did not examine any witnesses as our suit is title based. The defendant too examined just himself.

I finally get the news I was waiting for. I receive a letter from Fr. O'Brien informing me that the job is available. But I have to apply for a visa for which certain documents are required. A trip to Bombay becomes necessary. This time I travel alone to Bombay. It takes me ten days to obtain the documents which I mail to the authorities in Ireland.

Chapter 29

Judgement

Alberto is confident and upbeat about the case ruling being in his favour. The suit is coming for judgement the following day after two adjournments. The lawyer is certain the judgement will not be adjourned again, as the Judge is known to be prompt and rarely adjourns a judgement twice, unless it is particularly difficult. And never thrice. But our lawyer was cautious. Touch and go is what he said.

There is a slight drizzle as it happens when the monsoon is on its way out, when I hear a knock at the door. I open the door and a vaguely familiar figure is standing outside. I call him in. Alberto immediately recognises him and looks towards him in what appears to me, anticipation.

As he sits down, he says to Alberto, "I am sorry; your job could not be done. The Judge states that he tried to help you but could not overcome a particular difficulty."

He puts his hand in his pocket, takes out an envelope and

gives it to Alberto, who accepts it. He sits quietly with sadness on his face.

"The Judge was perturbed that he could not find a way to help you. He is a real gentleman, always performs as promised, either delivers a favourable judgement or refunds the amount. Otherwise I would not get involved."

As the man walks out, Alberto thanks him.

After he has left, Alberto looks dispirited.

"Don't you know him?" he questions me.

"I cannot recognize him," I say to him.

"You have seen him several times. Is he not the bailiff of the Court where our case is conducted?"

"Oh, I see. In the Court he usually wears the gown of the bailiff. I did not recognize him without it. But why did he come? And what is that he gave you"

"This is what happens when you are not at home but busy with your friends. He had come here a few days back on behalf of the Judge hearing the case. The Judge had sent him to tell me that the case can be decided in my favour if an amount of five thousand rupees is paid to him. I was in two minds. But then he assured me that in case the Judge cannot decide in my favour the money will be returned. So I thought, after we have spent so much, why must I not invest a little more to assure a win? Today, he has returned the same envelope which I had given him unopened. I appreciate at least this honesty of the Judge. Actually to be honest I had believed such things only happen elsewhere."

The judgement is fixed for the next day. But the hearing becomes irrelevant as we are aware of the negative judgement. Nevertheless, we proceed to the Court as our lawyer has called us.

There are three other matters fixed for judgement. The same bailiff calls out the first and the Judge announces "suit allowed".

The second suit the Judge says "suit partly allowed".

After that, the name of Alberto and Damião is called and the Judge pronounces "suit dismissed".

The Judge then looks at our lawyer and tells him, "I could not agree with you on the aspect of limitation, so the issue goes against you. Otherwise, there is merit in your case, you may read the judgement."

Our advocate takes the file and sits down to read. After some time he returns the file and comes out. We follow him.

"The judgement is more than fifty pages long. I have only read the relevant part. As I had feared, the issue of limitation has gone against us. But I did hope that my submissions and the citations provided would make a difference. I feel we could give it a try in the Court of the Judicial Commissioner by filing an appeal. After all we have come so far why not go a little further? I shall obtain a certified copy of the order. You can meet me after ten days."

We thank him and then Alberto mentions to him in passing. "At least the Judge is honest."

"Indeed he is, no one can question his honesty and integrity. But I may not say the same thing about his judicial ability," says our lawyer.

We reach home and soon Bhatkar comes over to find out the outcome of the case, as he has been diligently following the proceedings. He is not unduly surprised but is saddened by the outcome as he knows that Alberto is the real owner of the property in question.

"Judgements are often technical," he mentions.

"But it is injustice to us," retorts Alberto.

"Remember that there are no courts of justice here. These are merely courts of law."

"What then are courts of justice?" I ask.

"That is a huge question which I am not competent to answer. Our courts merely record evidence, hear submissions apply the law and pronounce judgements on the facts produced. Justice is something sublime which no Court in India is equipped to deliver."

At this point Alberto tells him about the return of the money by the Judge. The Bhatkar is stunned and looks in disbelief. "Are you speaking the truth? No one will believe that this particular Judge will do such a thing. He belongs to the old school. No scope for such double dealing with him. Besides he is so well-to-do and is self-respecting. Why would he stoop so low? Impossible to think so."

Alberto takes out the envelope with the money and shows it to him. Bhatkar remains silent.

Days later, we go to meet the lawyer at his office, accompanied by Bhatkar. As we sit in the office, our lawyer expresses his confidence that an appeal could reverse the judgement. He feels that the Judge may not have got the thrust of his argument, and a different Judge may have a different appreciation. He strongly suggests that an appeal may be filed in the Court of the Judicial Commissioner. We agree.

The Bhatkar then mentions to him about the return of the money. Our lawyer puts his elbows on his desk, places his face between his palms and just stares ahead without any comment for a long time. He then jumps up and almost shouts, "Not him. He will never do such a thing. We have grown up together. His background will never permit such conduct. I do not disbelieve you but there must be a catch somewhere. Needs to be investigated. Can you come to the Court tomorrow at four-thirty? Can you come with them?" He looks towards the Bhatkar, who nods.

The next day all three of us are sitting in the open court room. The court is recording evidence. Our lawyer arrives before the court closes. The Judge turns to him and questions, "Do you have any matter Advocate Borges?"

"No. But Your Honour I need a few words with you in your chamber."

As the Judge retires to his chamber, he calls our advocate in. We continue to sit in the court room. After about ten minutes we are called inside the chamber. Alberto narrates the happenings to the Judge and shows him the envelope with the money which he has brought as suggested by our advocate. The Judge turns pale on hearing it, and is virtually speechless.

The Judge summons the bench clerk and directs her to call the bailiff. He walks in jauntily but on seeing us he loses his nerve.

"Lucas" says the Judge to him. "Do you know this man?" (pointing towards Alberto).

The bailiff nods his head and then prostrates himself on the floor almost at the feet of the Judge and starts to cry.

"Save me, Sir, I will not repeat the mistake. I am at your mercy."

"What mistake? Do I know what mistake you have committed? First you tell me what is it that you have done? How can I save you unless I know what you need to be saved from? Stand up."

He slowly rises to his feet.

"I am sorry Sir. I am addicted to 'matka'* and all my salary goes there. So I had to devise a way to earn a little more."

"Either you tell me what you have been doing or I call the police right now. And see that you withhold nothing. I want the truth. And the absolute truth. If I believe you are not truthful, the police will be here at short notice. You do not have to be told about police ways. You will go in and remain in. Which Judge will give you bail?"

The bailiff is visibly shaken up and begins to shiver. He is struggling to maintain his balance. Finally he opens his mouth.

"Well, sitting in court, I keep track of suits that come for judgement. I follow the case and more or less from the submissions and Your Honour's expression one can make out

---

*A form of organised gambling

which way the judgement will go."

After a long pause he resumes: "When the final arguments are completed, I proceed to the house of the plaintiff and tell him that I have been sent by the Judge who is willing to decide in his favour, if a certain consideration is paid. Then I go to the defendants and repeat the same story. I also assure them that the Judge is an honourable man and the money will be returned if the matter is not decided in their favour. I take personal responsibility in this regard. Being an official of the court itself, the parties have no reason to doubt me.

As the judgement is dictated, I come to know which way the judgement has gone. I further confirm it from the steno. I proceed to the house of the party who has lost the case and return his money. The party usually is grateful that at least the money is returned. I also go to the other party's house and give them the good news. I usually get a reward."

All of us are astonished but at the same time impressed by the inventiveness of the bailiff.

"In how many cases have you followed this subterfuge?" The angry Judge questions.

"May be about fifteen cases."

"From this court?"

"No sir. From all courts."

"So you have made every Judge corrupt. Some sort of a consolation for me. Is it?"

No response as the bailiff puts his head down and remains silent.

"You have brought dishonor to the judiciary and to me personally. And do you call this a mistake? This is well planned and downright misuse of your position to bring disrepute to the Judiciary. No doubt there are frequent murmurs of corruption in the judiciary. What do you want me to do with you? Can such conduct be overlooked?"

The bailiff begins to cry as he pleads that he has a wife and children and that he will be a reformed man henceforth.

"I cannot condone such behavior. I will have to discuss the matter with my brother Judges. I have only two options, one is to lodge a complaint which is what I am thinking of doing. The other option is for you to hand over your resignation, upon which may be if the brother Judges agree, you could avoid criminal prosecution. I am making this suggestion to my brother Judges because otherwise you have been a good official. But I cannot assure you on this."

The bailiff is allowed to go. He walks out slowly.

The Judge appreciates our act. He says, "Just imagine if the suit was decided in your favour. You would believe you have purchased the order. And I would be corrupt, in your mind. It really is true that it takes all types to make the world. How devious can a mind be? If it was not brought to my notice it could go on and on," he concludes grimly as we take leave.

The Bhatkar and our lawyer walk down the stairs animatedly discussing the happenings. We cross the road in front, into the parking area. As discussed earlier with Bhatkar, we decide to file an appeal. And so we instruct our lawyer, who calls us to the office a week later. As we continue talking our lawyer remarks, "We are a dishonest people. See fifteen suits mean thirty litigants have paid the bailiff money to buy justice. So, fifteen have got the money back. They believe the Judge is honest. And the other fifteen are convinced that it is their money and not the efforts of their advocate or merits of the case that they have got the judgement. And they believe the Judge is dishonest. And that includes you Alberto."

"True sir," responds Alberto.

"It should never have happened. I ought not to have paid the money, I can see on hindsight. But one thing my negative act has had a positive effect though unwittingly."

Our lawyer concurs.

Chapter 30

The Proposal

"Now, that you are getting set to migrate to Ireland, is it not time for you to settle down?" asks Alberto. "After all once you reach there who knows how many pretty Irish lasses will be following you. Aren't you too handsome not to escape their attention?"

"Is it not too early for me to think of marriage?" I respond.

"It is not a matter of being early or late but of finding a girl from our own background. You have been brought up here in India and would it not be ideal for you to marry a local girl? I have broached this topic because I got the feeling that you and that soprano Celine from the choir seem to be attracted to each other. With your baritone and her soprano it should make for a harmonious combination. It is not?"

I blush at the suggestion, but I could not deny his inference.

"I would suggest that you both talk it over and may be you could proceed to Ireland and come back to get married. Should I talk to her?" asks the match maker.

'Go ahead," was my response.

Actually I was hoping someone other than me would take up the difficult task.

The following day, Alberto says he has spoken to her and she has strong feelings towards me which she confessed. "But she says the matter will have to be decided by her mother. So, I have offered to meet her mother along with you this Sunday after the nine o'clock Mass," Alberto says.

Dressed suitably, both of us cycle towards Celine's house which is about a kilometre away. The house has a wide façade with fluted columns and fretted windows enclosed within a high wall with a decorative gate. It is a big mansion, the type of which there are a few in the village. We are welcomed at the door by Celine who takes us into the sitting room and offers us seats. The sitting room is large, painted light cream with old furniture, the type no longer being made. A piano stands in the corner. A twelve-arm chandelier hangs from the teak wood ceiling. Framed photographs adorn the walls.

"That is my father," says Celine, as she points to a photograph of a gentleman with a stern look on his visage.

Soon her mother, whom we have seen but never met, gives a benign smile and makes us feel welcome as she sits down. Celine takes a seat by her side. After some time she goes in and returns with cups of steaming coffee and some snacks.

"The first time I saw you, in church," she says to Alberto, "you reminded me of my brother. Your voice sounds so much like his. Physically you are portly and with a receding hairline. But that is what happens with age. The last time I saw my brother, he was slim with a head full of hair. But there is an uncanny resemblance between my brother and you. And you hold the violin just the way my brother used to."

"Where is your brother?" interjects Alberto.

"I wish I knew. My brother worked on the ship. During the

war, the ship was sunk but it was said that there were survivors. However, there was no information about my brother. All that, was many years ago. I presume he is dead as otherwise, I am sure he would have somehow contacted his parents and his sister."

"Was his name Alberto?"

"Indeed it was."

"How do you know?"

"I am just asking. Now tell me Maria, as a small child, aged four or five, were you ever lost at Crawford Market and traced the following day?" questions Alberto.

"Very much so," says Maria.

'Now do you remember that Alberto was suspended from his school ANZAs because he put itching powder on the chair of a teacher?"

"That is true."

"Well, not only do I look and sound like Alberto but I *am* Alberto. The ship did sink. But I survived. The rest is a long story which I will keep for another day," says Alberto.

Maria is stunned at the revelation and for a moment is lost. She soon recovers her composure and hugs Alberto and holds on to him for a long time. We remain silent.

After sometime they separate and both sit on a sofa together holding hands. By and by Maria opens up to Alberto.

"After you went on your last trip before the ship sank, things changed totally for me. You know that Imtiaz, the tall and handsome boy from the slums of Agripada who was the star of the YMCA/NNH basketball team. Well, I fell in love with him and much against my parents wishes I eloped and married him. Your ship was reported sunk around the same time, earlier or later I do not recollect. Our parents completely disassociated themselves from us and would not even look at me," she paused.

After a brief moment, she resumed her narration.

"I went to live with Imtiaz in the slum. His basketball days were over and he did not have a steady job. He worked as a mechanic or welder, whenever a job offer came. Otherwise, the locality was seedy with all sorts of characters not particularly conducive to a good life. My husband's friends were mostly unsettled, and we were hard up."

"A son was born to us after two years. When the child was about three, another bout of the not so infrequent and infamous Bombay riots flared up. Gangs of people attacked our slum and murdered everybody in sight before the locality could take up defense. The attack was well planned. My husband was caught and murdered right in front of my eyes, in broad daylight and the slum was set on fire. The police simply looked on or supported the rioters. As the violence continued to grow everybody ran away. My son was lost. Actually if my husband had survived a few weeks, he would be in Iraq where his uncle had secured him a job as a driver. The visa arrived soon after he was killed."

"After wandering aimlessly, I ended up at a convent where I was given shelter for a few months. I spent week after fearful week, searching for my son in every nook and corner of Bombay. But he was gone. I only prayed to God to spare him. I always remember him. He was fair and chubby. If he has survived, he must be a handsome young man somwhere. After normalcy returned, I took a train to Goa. Our parents had in the meantime died one after the other from grief at the loss of their son and the living loss of their daughter. I had no face before our close relatives."

I looked on in trepidation.

"What was the name of your son?" enquired Alberto.

"I wish I could remember. Over the years, I have tried to recollect it but in my sorrow at the loss of my husband and son, I also forgot his name."

"Was it Ismael by any chance?" asks Alberto.

"I guess so, I guess so. Yes I remember, he was given a name which is common to both Islam and Christianity by my husband to signify the Christian/Muslim parentage of the child. Yes. It was Ismael."

Alberto stands up and says to her, "My beloved sister, I present Ismael to you." He turns to me, "Meet your mother, Ismael."

He looks at me. Now it is my turn to hug my mother. I say to myself I had come looking for a mother-in-law and I find my mother. And lose a prospective wife. What a situation!

Celine on the other hand had realised the implications and was in tears, perhaps both of happiness because her mother had found her brother and son and sadness because she could not marry the man she loved. Our plans had gone bust.

We sat and continued to make small talk for some time. Before taking leave we were invited for dinner, the following Sunday, in view of our newly confirmed relationship. So now almost from thin air, I found a mother and an uncle and lost a potential wife.

Celine came to drop us till the front gate of the compound. She hugged me as she said she may have to join the Apostolic Carmel as a nun. And I was contemplating the Society of Jesus. After all, had I not been part of the Society from childhood?

ɔ

Chapter 31

The Nuptials

Life in Goa is slow and sedate. The process of marriage is likewise languorous though entertaining.

Registration of a marriage has several pre-requisites. The bride has to be over 18 years and the groom over 21 years to be eligible to register a marriage. We produce the birth certificate of Celine. My birth is not registered as there is no compulsory registration of births in Bombay. I rely upon my baptism certificate. But we have to return from the registry because a residence certificate of either the bride or the groom is needed. I am not eligible for a residence certificate as I do not have a ration card in my village. I did not make one because it entailed the cancellation of my card in Bombay.

It is Celine who applied for her residence certificate at her Village Panchayat. But for days no certificate is forthcoming despite the fact that all necessary documents have been produced. No reason is given for the delay. Maria has made several visits to the office and as also the residence of the

Sarpanch. Every time she is assured the certificate will be ready, shortly, but it never materialises.

Frustrated by the delay Alberto takes charge and speaks to the Sarpanch but meets with the same lethargy. The Secretary informs Alberto that the certificate has to be issued by the Sarpanch and he has kept the letterheads and the seal with him at home. He sends Maria and me to the residence of the Sarpanch. The Sarpanch keeps us sitting for an hour before he comes out. But still the certificate is not ready. He still has some excuse not to provide it.

As we talk Alberto arrives bringing with him a big "ganton*" of assorted fish with, mullets, ladyfish, perch and pomfrets on prominent display. Alberto greets the Sarpanch whose eyes widen, looking at the string of prized fresh fish.

As he sits down, the Sarpanch says, "Why did you have to come? The certificate is getting ready. I have to merely sign and stamp it."

"Thank you," Alberto says as he asks, "Where is Paulo the cook?

"He is inside. You may go in."

Alberto goes in with the fish. But before that, he invites the Sarpanch for dinner the same evening. "I will exit from the rear door. Please collect the certificate," he says aloud to us.

The Sarpanch is soon busy with the certificate which is in fact a printed form with only the details of the person needing to be filled in. It is signed, stamped and given to us. I put the certificate in my pocket close to my heart. I drop Maria at her residence and give the certificate to Celine. And we sit down and talk. I have lunch with them. They will be joining us for dinner later in the evening. By the time I arrive home, Alberto is having a nap after lunch.

---

* fish on a string

By six o'clock Alberto is occupied with the fish which he has already cleaned and marinated. By eight, a few close neighbours invited for the dinner begin to arrive. And that includes the Bhatkar. As he sits down, he queries.

"How did it go? Did you get the certificate?"

"Went perfectly," responds Alberto with a loud laugh. "We will know the rest after Paulo joins us."

"Sit down. Since you do not drink what do I offer you?" "Bring a Coke," responds Bhatkar.

Paulo enters a few minutes later with a broad smile on his face.

"How was the aftermath?" questions Alberto.

"Half an hour after you left I was called in by the Sarpanch", and he says:

'I want the pomfret *recheado**. See that the masala is proper and not too pungent as you did with the mackerels some days back when my mother-in-law was here. She even believes that it was maliciously done to keep her away from coming over. My wife was furious with you and me'.

"Fine, I will take care. I will use fewer chillies and more sugar, I said as I went back to the kitchen."

"I return to see him after some time asking for money to buy pomfrets from the market. "What did you do with the fish?"he asks in anger.

"Which fish?"

'The fish that Alberto brought.'

'What can I do with Alberto's fish? He entered the kitchen, invited me for dinner and went out through the rear door. In fact I am going there for dinner tonight. I believe he has invited you too. Are you coming? We will then know what he has done with the fish. The fish really looked fresh and appetizing as he carried it back with him.'

"You should have seen his face. He let loose a string of

---

* Stuffed with masala

expletives, such as I had never before heard or knew existed. See that you do not rub him the wrong way," he advises.

The Bhatkar and Alberto break out in fits of uncontrolled laughter.

"Was this your advice?" Paulo asks Bhatkar.

"Do you think Alberto needs any advice?"

"Do you know something?" asks Paulo.

Alberto looks blankly at him.

"That Salvador Nunes landlord from Cortalim twice came to see the Sarpanch. They were talking of Celine and her marriage. I could not hear everything but I feel the delay in issuing the residence certificate has something to do with his visits."

But that was not the end of hurdles on our way to the altar. After getting the Residence Certificate we still had a mountain to climb. The reading of the first of the three banns in the churches resulted in heightened activity. It soon became clear that at least two or three families had their eyes on the bride, if not for her, then for her considerable estate. She being the only child the marriage would be matri-local. Among the prospective grooms was a distant cousin of the bride's father. Immediately, attempts began to be made to dissuade Celine from marrying me, the son of a slum dwelling Muslim from Bombay of unknown pedigree. Fortunately, Celine was with me and the mother could not have any objections to her own son's wedding on ground of pedigree or whatever.

Objections were raised with the Parish Priest by Salvador Nunes, who also went to the former Regedor* who took them to a leading lawyer in Margao. The lawyer after verifying the facts advised that there is no legal impediment to the marriage. The crestfallen objectors had to retreat.

The actual preparations for the nuptials begin a few days before the scheduled date with a *Bikareanchem Jevonn** . Essentially it involves inviting the poor for a meal at which

---

* Meal to the poor

they sit and recite the rosary and other prayers in memory of the dead ancestors of the house. The prayers are followed by a meal offered to them. As they leave they are also given some amount of cash.

And then comes the *'roce'* generally two or three days before the nuptials. It involves rituals where coconuts are ground and the juice extracted is collected in a copper vessel. The well wishers and friends of the groom are then all invited usually in the evening time. The groom sits down and the coconut milk is poured over him, cup by cup by those present. Songs specially meant for the occasion are sung. Some eggs are also broken on the head of the groom and allowed to drip over him. By the end, the groom is a dripping mess. After the ceremony, the groom has a bath, gets dressed and attends the ceremonial meal provided to all those present. A similar ceremony takes place at the bride's place. The whole ceremony actually signals the end of the single life of the bride and the groom. On the wedding day, a relative of the groom takes the trousseau to be worn at the nuptials to the bride's house. As I have only my uncle Alberto who has other duties, my friend Roque fulfills the role. Alberto has got the gold found in his father's trunk polished till it glitters like new. The bride is then dressed. As she is ready to leave the house, relatives and neighbours come over to bless her. Photographs are taken as the bride along with the bridesmaids, flower girls, parents, and relatives leave the house for the Church.

We are now waiting outside the church for the priest to come to the door and lead us to the altar. Normally the groom is led to the altar by the mother and the bride by the father. In my case, it is Alberto who leads me to the altar, while Celine is led by Joaquim another distant cousin of her father. As I watch him, I can see he is stiff and seems to be doing a task forced upon him. I later learn that he too had interest in Celine for his son and therefore the discomfort.

The nuptials go on smoothly. Our own choir led by Alberto is at its very best and put their heart and soul into the hymns.

Celine and I sing the Ave Maria in unison. We sign the register of marriage at the altar with a witness from either side attesting.

We move outside the church where the invitees have all queued up and are eager to wish us. One by one we are hugged and kissed, until darkness sets in. We move over to our house. As we enter the house, the mandatory psalm *Laudate*, adapted and set to music by Wolfgang Mozart, is sung with Alberto leading the chorus:

Laudate Dominum omnes gentes

Laudate eum, omnes populi

Quoniam confirmata est

Super nos misericordia eius

Et veritas, veritas Domini manet, manet in aeternum

Gloria Patri et Filio

Et Spiritui Sancto

Sicut erat in principio

Et nunc, et semper

Et in saecula saeculorum

Amen, Amen, Amen, Amen.

Nuptials over, we move to the house of Celine with its spacious halls and accommodation, for the reception.

Chapter 32

The Toast

The band has come all the way from Siolim with its reputation as the very best in the territory – Johnson and his Jolly Boys. The caterer, Pascoal, has come from Panjim. The best in the business too. Maria says that is the way George would do it. No expenses spared.

The reception begins with the wedding march, culminating in us coming to the centre of the hall. A round table with the wedding cake awaits us. The cake is in the shape of a harp the national symbol of Ireland, a country where we are going to settle, after the nuptials.

"Just two hours earlier Ismael and Celine entered the Church as bride and groom. And now here they are before us all resplendent and happy as they take their first steps together as husband and wife," announces the Master of Ceremonies. He goes on, *"No celebration in Goa is complete unless a cake is cut, champagne uncorked and a toast raised. And we are going*

to have all three. We begin with the cake. At the countdown of three the bride and the groom will hold the knife and make the ceremonial cut. Three – Two – One."

We cut the cake to loud applause with the band too leading with *Congratulations and Celebrations*

"The time to uncork the champagne has come. And to do the honours we have Alberto, the groom's uncle, who says he would do so regularly during his days as seaman, but has now lost touch. Here he comes," announces the Master of Ceremonies.

Alberto holds the bottle shakes it up and down like a professional and pops it open, first try, spilling froth all over. The glasses are filled and distributed.

"And now to raise the toast we have a very well known personality and a close friend of both the families The Bhatkar."

The Bhatkar steps out to loud applause.

It is my joy and my pride to raise this toast to Ismael and his bride, Celine. Congratulations to both of you. And to your families.

Hope springs eternal from the human breast, it has been wisely said. And we have witnessed today the triumph of hope over despair. The groom was full of hope when he accompanied Alberto to the house of Maria to seek the hand of Celine in marriage. Pretty soon storm clouds covered the sky and the first gust of wind blew their hopes away. Ismael and Alberto slowly retraced their steps hit by the tragic-comic turn of events. Ismael considered joining the Society of Jesus, which has played a prominent role in his growth. And Celine nearly ended up joining the Apostolic Carmel where her aunt is a Mother Superior. And for reasons, beyond their or anyone else's comprehension.

The ill wind blew away as quickly as it had come. The clouds disappeared and a clear blue sky smiled. And hope triumphed over despair. And that is how this young couple marched to the altar today.

The young couple does not need my advice. They are competent and capable of managing their own affairs. But I will love to speak on things that the young couple may encounter as they grow from a young couple into a well knit family. To begin with I will go into Greek mythology.

"Well, most of us have heard of Pandora's Box. For those of you who have not aware, let me elucidate: Pandora was, according to the myth, the first woman on Earth. She was created by the gods; each one of them gave her a gift, thus, her name in Greek means "the one who bears all gifts. All these gifts were put in a box or a jar, called "pithos" in Greek. The gods told her that the box contained special gifts from them. The lid was tightly closed and presented to Pandora with instructions that the box be never opened.

Pandora was trying to tame her curiosity, but at the end, she could not hold herself anymore; she opened the box and all the illnesses and hardships that the gods had hidden in the box started coming out. Pandora was scared, because she saw all the evil spirits coming out and tried to close the box as fast as possible, closing Hope inside.

The gods it is said wanted to let people suffer in order to understand that they should not disobey their gods. Pandora was the right person to do it, because she was curious enough, but not malicious"

So the implication for you Ismael is clear, when you have Celine with you, hope is with you. The woman that she is, she will be curious but not malicious. When things do go wrong, and sometime they indeed will, you will still have hope with you. And so long as hope is with you, a better tomorrow will beckon. So take good care of her. Keep her safe. Look after her, love and protect her. Because hope lies in her and with her.

Here in India a woman is brought up to believe that her husband is god. And a woman treats her husband, as such. She even walks a step behind her husband. As you settle down you will find that Celine places before you food, that is overdone and burnt. But you must not conclude that she is no good in the kitchen. That really is not so. In fact I can testify that both Celine and her mother are great cooks for I have dined at their home in the past.

I will request you to revisit the Old Testament. And you will read that God came down to earth in a cloud of fire and men placed burnt offerings before him. That is what happens with a bride during the honeymoon period. She treats her husband as the God of the Old Testament and places burnt offerings before him. But this will pass. Soon your wife will realise that her husband is no God but just another mortal! And it is then that you will get all that tasty food. And well done. You may then invite me for lunch or dinner!

And now this is to both of you. We Indians are a cricket crazy people. When a match is on, life comes to a standstill. You will find married life is like a cricket match. Ismael, as I know him, is a fast bowler. There will be days when he will come charging in fast and furious and bowling short. Normally Celine you must swerve or duck and allow the ball to go harmlessly by. But sometimes the bouncers become too many. At such times you must be prepared to hook or pull and send the ball flying over the boundary. Nothing chastises a fast bowler more than being ruthlessly hit. Things will return to normal,soon.

But Ismael you may have a more difficult time at the crease when Celine has the ball in her hands. No, she will not come charging at you. For, she is a lady. She will come with a smile on her lips roll her arms over and deliver. And you will not know whether it is a googly or a Chinaman or whatsoever. The ball will do something you never imagined it could and hit the wicket. Head down you will have to walk to the pavilion. But of course there is always a second innings. Marriage, after all is a test match, not a one day international!

"Wives of course have irritating ways sometimes. Imagine you are on a holiday. You are half way to the destination. Your wife will tap you and ask sweetly, Did you put off the iron? Of course you do not remember clearly. You have doubts. But you say yes I did put it off. The rest of the trip you are haunted by doubts. Did I put off the iron? But your wife does not really believe you. She knows your ways and your answers. So the next day she casually queries when does the fire insurance expire? You say there is time for it. Actually you do not know. The result is that your entire holiday has gone up in smoke. So I suggest when you go on a trip do carry the iron with you. It then does not matter whether the power button is on or off. Besides, it will help iron out any differences that may arise on the trip!

"And finally, let me take you to the beginning. Genesis. Chapter1:28. After Adam and Eve had disobeyed God they were banished from the Garden of Eden. And God said to them. Go forth and multiply. Ever since, man has been multiplying. And we Goans have been following the advice.

But there is a problem. Despite the multiplication, the population of our community on this red soil of Goa is declining year after year. The Church is complaining that young men are not joining the priesthood. But where are the young men? Soon there will be churches but none to attend them. It is already happening in Bardez. And without us, Goa will never be Goa. Nothing wrong to go abroad to earn but you must return to your roots. Sadly that is not happening. After your working life is over wherever you are remember, that the Lord only said "Go forth and multiply." But the Lord never said "Multiply and Go"! You have a duty to your mother land to come back.

And remember one more thing. A happy marriage does not mean you do not get angry with or do not find fault with or do not quarrel with or do not get cross with each other. No. Not at all. A happy marriage means all these unsavoury things do happen but you resolve them quickly and amicably.

And continue with life as if none of these things have happened.

You have been patient. I do not wish to take more of your time. Neither more of the time of the invitees gathered here. Here is wishing the bridal couple all the best that life has to offer, health, happiness and prosperity. And a large brood of children, If I may say so. May the good Lord bless and keep you together now and always. Cheers.

Chapter 33

The Corrigendum

Being a little mischievous, I believe is a natural part of everyone's make up. And the same with me, perhaps a little more. I have consciously put you in the situation where you presently find yourself. The doubts that have germinated in your mind after going through the narrative are well founded. I concede I have withheld relevant and material information. You may even feel it is done on purpose. My sincere apologies to you as I take you back to what you have missed.

I had to travel from Goa to Bombay to tie up the loose ends, obtain all my certificates and then proceed to Delhi. It took three trips to Delhi before our visas were stamped by the Embassy of Ireland. And the marriage had to be hurried as Celine would otherwise, not be eligible to travel with me.

After our first meeting, when our relationship with Maria came to be known, we were invited for dinner. As we arrive, we see Maria all aflutter to provide the best ambience, food and drink to her long lost brother and new-found son. The twelve

-arm chandelier is lit. The lamps on the wall are aglow. Even George's portrait on the wall seemed to have a smile on his face rather than the stern look which I had noticed on our first visit. All is bright and cheerful. Except Celine.

Celine looks a complete contrast to her usual vibrant self. There are shadows under her eyes. The rosy glow in her cheeks is replaced by a sallow countenance. I have never seen her so depressed. The sadness cannot be hidden, although she does make a brave attempt to look normal. My sadness is nothing less. But no external display. I suppose being brought up as an orphan helps you to conceal your feelings.

Maria (I cannot bring myself to call her mother yet) holds Alberto by the hand and leads him into the cellar. We follow. It is a dark little room now lit by two chimney lamps. The entry to it, is by a stairway leading down.

"I do not know anything about wines. My husband had stocked it in his days as captain, before I had married him. You may pick whichever you fancy," she looks at us.

Alberto hesitates for a moment. He then inspects the bottles systematically lined up. He picks one up and gives it to me. We climb up. The label reads Warre's Founded in 1670 Portugal.

Back in the sitting room. Albert opens the bottle and pours it into a wine glass a little below the brim. He pours a little for me in another and insists that I try it.

"It is a good vintage. You may not get it elsewhere," offers Alberto.

Being a non drinker it means little to me but I have to sip it. Civility says so.

Alberto sips the wine leisurely as he observes. "It takes me back to my days on the ship when good wine flowed easy."

Presently we get back to where our conversation had ended on the earlier occasion.

"You have not told us what happened after the death of your husband and how you landed in Goa. I do hope you did have an easier time than I had," says Alberto.

Maria begins: 'I arrived in Goa, completely empty handed with only a few clothes which the nuns had provided me. I had nowhere to go as my aunt in Goa had cut me off because of my ill-fated marriage. The deaths of my parents had further hardened her attitude towards me.

"However, I had to swallow my pride and make my way to my aunt Cynthia who lived in Margao. She failed to ackowledge me, initially. But on seeing my plight she was quite civil and welcomed me. Her husband had expired and her children were abroad. In a way, my presence helped and provided her company in her old age. But, she never failed to remind me of my indiscipline and ingratitude towards my parents which she claimed, not without justification, was the main cause of their premature deaths. There was not much I could do in such moments. Otherwise also, she gradually became very cantankerous and unbearable, more so after her son in the United States paid for a maid to care for her. I was feeling frustrated and even suicidal.

But I did not wish to succumb to such notions, so I felt I must locate our house at Calata. I travelled by train as I knew a pathway led to our house. My plan was to start a tailoring shop and teach knitting and embroidery to eke out a living. I clearly remembered the path to our house along the bund by the side of Tolleabund pond a straight walk from the railway station. I soon reached our house. I was so happy to see it. Recalling the good times we had when down during the vacation brought tears to my eyes. Our house was in good condition but locked. I contacted Rosario the neighbour who directed me to the house of Damião my father's godchild, who was holding the keys to the house. He was abrupt and downright hostile and fabricated a story that he had made the full payment to my father to purchase the house and that therefore he is the owner. Only the sale deed was not executed, he claimed. Nevertheless, he offered to pay me an amount of Rs 1,500 if I would sign the deed confirming the sale. I am certain that my father would never sell the house as he had plans to return to Goa and settle down. He loved the place and constantly talked of spending his last days among childhood friends. I declined his offer. He doubled it. As I had no help, I just remained silent and walked away".

"During this period I was a regular at the church. I would also assist the nuns of Apostolic Carmel who ran a school in the town and one of the nuns was well disposed towards me. She called me one day and suggested that I could be a nanny to a little girl who was her niece and whose mother had expired at childbirth. Her brother just could not cope up with the situation. I looked upon it as a God-sent opportunity.

Thus, I ended up at this large mansion in this village. The child looked divine and I was happy to take care of her. She provided me with a distraction from my regular moments of despair at the way my life had unfolded. Gradually, I became completely attached to the child and she considered me as her mother as she had not seen any other. But I did feel lost in this massive labyrinthine house."

After a pause she resumes the narrative. "The man of the house looked grave and serious. I learnt that he had avoided marriage for years until his sister practically forced him into it as he had no other siblings except the nun. Sadly for him, his wife died too soon.

He was a good father to the extent that he met all the needs of his daughter. But there never was the father-daughter relationship that little girls have with their father. He was completely aloof from the child and was always in his own world. His friends would come over and they were engrossed in their own discussions or in playing cards and drinking.

By the time Celine had grown up into a young lady, I began to see that her father became a little friendlier towards me. He began to talk and seemed to enjoy my company. And the relationship of employer and employee had gone. He had got over the unexpected loss of his wife, I began to think."

She perks up as she continues "For the first time, one rainy day in the month of August, he suggested that we attend a movie at Cine Vishant in Margao. 'It is a wonderful movie. I had seen it in New York soon after it was released'

"George, I must mention was a master mariner. I readily agreed as I have not seen a movie for years. The theatre was crowded but he had managed to get three balcony tickets in advance. The movie was engrossing and the best I have ever seen. As we sat he began to softly caress my hands. Soon he put his arms around my shoulders. I felt warm and comfortable and did not do anything to discourage him. I was quite familiar with the music and the songs in the film, which I have taught Celine and who sings them so well."

She stops for breath before contiuing, "the movie got over by about nine o'clock. It continued to rain as we drove back and he parked the car outside the popular restaurant Longuinhos, generally considered to be the best place in town, to eat out. We took corner seats in the family room. The restaurant soon filled up with diners. I was feeling like I had never felt for so many years. He ordered a beer for himself. It was a coke each for me and Celine. We sat silently just looking at each other. He seemed a totally changed man.

He took almost half an hour to order dinner. The food arrived, another half an hour later. Except for one table, everyone else had dined and left. By the time we had finished we were the only ones left.

I could see that he wished to say something but was struggling for the right words. Perhaps he wanted the other diners to leave. In the end he blurted out. 'Don't you think it is time we have a sequel, a real life sequel, to the movie?' I was overwhelmed, but not surprised having watched him in recent months. Truth to say, I had been developing feelings for him but did not know how to express them".

I could only respond, "what will the world say?

"Forget the world. What do you say?

"It was now my turn to struggle for words. I just looked at him with watery eyes. But I managed to say, you are George and I am Maria. Even the names are the same. Yes, why not? Destiny must have had a hand in this. He stood up and hugged me. Celine looked at us with an amused smile. He had chosen the best possible way to bring up the subject".

"The ride back home was heavenly. I had never felt so light hearted, so happy, since the sad happenings in Bombay. The tide had turned, for the better, I felt."

"Have you seen the movie?" she asks me.

"Which one?"

"I have provided enough clues," she smiles.

"Love story?" I am tentative.

'It is a love story but not 'The Love Story", she teases.

"Is it Dr. Zhivago?"

"There is no Maria in there. Only Lara. And Celine loves the theme. She plays it wonderfully well on the piano."

"I am at a loss. What movie could it be?" I say to myself.

"The Sound of Music," she opens up.

"What an idiot am I?" I say aloud.

"It was so evident. Was it not?"

"How did I not get it? Of course, of course I know all the songs."

"So do I. And so does Celine. And she sings them so well too."

"We performed it at our school annual," I say defensively.

She continues, "We were married within a matter of two months in a private ceremony, attended by his very close family members. My aunt had expired in the meantime, thus there was no family member present from my side. Celine was the bridesmaid. And so began our new life. But it was short lived. My marriage though flitting was blissful and contented. I was destined to be a widow. Destiny has stayed with me through times, good and bad. But I have been blessed with Celine who is more than a daughter to me. My final wish is to see her settled with a nice boy.

I look at Celine who is confused. Maria hugs her tight.

'No matter what, I will be your mother as I always have been," she sobs quietly.

As they separate, Celine walks towards me and embraces me.

"What does it mean? Do we continue to be brother and sister? Does it make any difference?"

"I believe it does. The Apostolic Carmel may lose a potential Mother Superior. And the Jesuits may lose a priest." She gets it and her joy is boundless. Still we may have to seek proper legal opinion.

"But could you not have disclosed earlier that Maria was not your biological mother?".

"A mother, I thought was a mother. How would I know that it would make a difference?"

And now it is Alberto's turn to be match-maker. "Now tell me will your son be a nice boy for Celine?"

"Which son?"

"Your only son."

"Why was I kept in the dark all the while?"

"Where was the chance at all?" asks Alberto.

"Once you identified yourself it was clear you are the real mother of the prospective groom. And until today the prospective bride was your biological daughter. So how could they ever marry?"

"But can they marry now?" she inquires

"I believe so, but we can verify. Do you give your consent?"

"If Celine agrees, I have no problem."

"But now that I am your son do I have your consent to marry Celine?" I tease her.

The dinner table is set for twelve. It is long and rounded at the ends. We occupy the middle seats. Maria and Celine on one side. We two on the opposite. Maria explains the vacant chairs. "The table has been set in this format, ever since I stepped in to the house. George did not want to alter it. He would say that the table has remained so since before he was born and he did not want to disturb the family tradition.For some reason he never occupied the head seat.And I do not want to disturb the tradition either. I never sat at this table until our marriage. I had my breakfast lunch and dinner at a side table in the kitchen, before that."

The table is laid with appetizing dishes.

"This is chicken cafreal, that is guisado[1], and here is pork vindalho[2]. The next is apa de camarão[3]. The cafreal was brought to Goa by the black soldiers from Mozambique in the Portuguese army and is now a Goan culinary delight," Maria points out.

"That over there is feijoada[4] with beans and sausages. Besides there is mackerel recheado, fish curry, sorpotel and vegetable dishes. Try them all."

We can see that she has spared no effort to provide a sumptuous meal.

She continues, "This bebinca[5] and all the desserts have been prepared by Celine. You must try them all."

But more much more than that, was my joy to see the colour return to Celine's face. The shadows under her eyes formed over a period of a week have disappeared in a trice. She is vivacious as ever. And so am I. No lunch or dinner had ever tasted better.

This narration opens the doors for our marriage. Celine did not know till this moment that a step daughter may marry her mother's biological son. I was not too sure either.

"You have no blood relationship to act as impediment to the marriage," confirms the *Padre Vigario.*

The same opinion is confirmed by our lawyer. The doors

---

1. dish of chopped meat
2. pork cooked in red masala with vinegar
3. prawn pie
4. dish with sausages and beans
5. layered cake made of coconut milk and egg yolks

are wide open.

So on the fifteenth of May we walk down the aisle. The lady who was to be my mother-in-law turns out to be my mother. And mother-in-law too! I do hope your doubts about an incestuous marriage have been cleared fully and finally.

Days after our marriage we get heart-warming news. Alberto could not be happier. The Court of the Judicial Commissioner at Panaji has allowed the appeal, set aside the Judgement and decree of the trial court and declared Alberto as owner of the property. Our advocate has done a commendable job. He had to make several trips to Panaji to argue the appeal. And we are obliged to him.

How do we thank him? Bhatkar tells us he is a connoisseur of wines. We gift him a good part of the vintage wine from Maria's cellar as an expression of our love and happiness at the wonderful manner in which he argued the case and won it for us.

Damião contacts Bhatkar and offers to deliver the property to Alberto without the need to file the execution application if he is compensated for his investment in the property. The matter is discussed with the Bhatkar who advises a settlement particularly because we are shortly leaving for Ireland and there may not be anyone here to handle the affairs. Our advocate advises us to file an Execution Application in which consent terms could be filed. By the end of the month the formalities are completed and the property is delivered to us. Before leaving, we enter into an agreement to sell the property to the son of the neighbour Rosario who offers a good price and advances earnest money towards the sale consideration. We execute a power of attorney in favour of Bhatkar to sign the deed, after we have received the balance of the sale consideration in Ireland from the buyer, who is a seaman, when his ship docks in that country.

Chapter 34

At Last

Farewell. A time to look behind. And it has come. It is now and here. Time to bid adeus to my friends who have made my life here, in this little village of Calata, so memorable. I have learnt the simple joys of living and giving. People are poor but not depraved. A place where poverty itself enriches you. The sun rises and the sun sets. Every day. And every week. The next day is no different from the previous. Neither the next week. If there is no food in the pot just take a walk. Fruits and wild berries abound. Or take a machete; you may find a beehive. Just cut into the tree and scoop it up. Or climb a coconut tree and pluck tender coconuts. Only take care the landlord is not within sight! Or dig into the drying muck of a pond and pick up the tasty and nutritious bulbs of the pond lily or lotus. You may eat them raw. And in season you freely get cashews aplenty. And you do not have to look out for the landlord! No one cares; you may take as many as you can eat. Only leave the nuts behind. And mangoes and jackfruits too. Or you can cook the leaves of so many wild shrubs into a tasty bhaji. And satiate your hunger. Or you locate a tortoise or two. Or catch fish. Or kill a bird or two as David slayed Goliath. If still hungry, a neighbour will gladly offer you a plate of fish curry and rice. Little demands easily fulfilled. Poor land where no one dies of hunger.

But how does one say farewell to such a heavenly place? And to whom do I say farewell? My friends, the football players, the bird-catchers the watermelon prize winners; yes why not? But where do I say farewell to them? Have they come to bid farewell to me? Not at all. Why not? Because they themselves have bid farewell one by one, over these few years.

And it is the same story generation after generation. Every young man yearns to cross the seas; every advertisement for jobs abroad is answered. Every agent is contacted; every contact is activated. And one fine day the visa arrives. And then like the mallards that fly down to Goa in winter, young men spring into action and fly. All, hoping to turn their winter into summer, like the avians. Roque is in Kuwait, Caetano is in Dubai. Luis, Francis, and Domingos are on board the ship. The rest are somewhere there in the big, wide, world. José is the only one here. No more does he provide flowers to the florists. He now runs his own restaurant catering to the needs of the hippies who too have heard of the goodness of the land and its people. And are now flooding the beaches. And like all my friends, I too was in the queue for the visa. I have now reached the front.

But we have the choir in which Celine and I are the lead singers. We owe it to the parish to give them a resounding farewell. And the parish turns out in full. The choir has thoughtfully choreographed the show which begins with a rendition of "It's a long way to Tipperary" and concludes with a heartrending farewell song composed by Edgar the local musical talent. It brings copious tears to our eyes. We can see that the Choir will really miss the choir master. And both of us, too.

And finally, we sing the farewell song from the movie that acted as a catalyst to bring my mother and my late father-in-law together. Both bear the same names in life as the protagonists in the movie. It was certainly destiny that had brought them together. And destiny that took George away before he could meet his son-in-law.

So long, farewell, auf wiedersehen, good night
I hate to go and leave this pretty sight

So long, farewell, auf wiedersehen, adieu
Adieu, adieu, to you and you and you

So long, farewell, au revoir, auf wiedersehen
I'd like to stay and taste my first champagne

So long, farewell, auf wiedersehen, goodbye
I leave and heave a sigh and say "Goodbye", goodbye

I'm glad to go, I cannot tell a lie
I flit, I float, I fleetly flee, I fly
Goodbye, Goodbye, Goodbye.

What will be the fate of the great ancestral mansion of my wife? And what will happen to the modest house Alberto purchased in my name? Will these houses turn into ruins the way of the ruined houses that I have seen in every village? Will someone say that the houses have collapsed because of the sins of the owners or their ancestors? Or will someone say that the owners migrated and prospered so much that this estate meant nothing to them? Or will someone claim to be mundkar? Or will some caretaker claim adverse possession? Or will some law take away the estates of all those who have gone abroad? How do I bid farewell to Agostinho, the tribal elder from Nuvem, and Reis Magos, the elder of the fishing community from Betalbatim, and their great wisdom? How can I ever forget the wonderful lilt in their narrative? These are questions that continue to haunt me.

And what about the land itself? Will it remain pristine and clean? The signs are worrying. The people are losing their simple innocent ways. But perhaps as Alberto says the progress of progress cannot be halted.

We attend a farewell Mass. Celine and my mother (oh yes my mother) go to the cemetery and lay a wreath at the family grave.

We stand by. All of us say a silent prayer. The flow of tears is endless.

Our bags are packed. Our tickets are confirmed. I am ready to go on a jet-plane. And with Celine in my arms. No need for her to wait for my return. As we drive to the airport, we zoom past the countryside which I have come to love over these many years. I look out wistfully with teary eyes at the land and memories I leave behind. And sigh. A latter day Boabdil!

...... And looking ahead.

It is cold almost freezing as we climb down the stairway on to the tarmac. A quick walk and we are within the lounge, warm and comforting. Visas are checked, passports are stamped. Fr O'Brien is waiting outside the arrival terminal. A quick hug and introduction to my family follow. We load our luggage, jump into the van. A long drive in the darkness of the night and we land at a monastery on the fringes of Dublin.

Arrangements have been made for our temporary stay. The sun is way up in the sky as we wake up after a tiring journey and try to overcome the jet lag.

A week after arriving we are back to our normal selves. No signs of jet lag. We are adapting to the weather. We have boarded the van and are driving from Dublin, South towards our destination. It is my first glimpse of what I have read as autumn colours. Green overlaid with vivid yellow, orange, red and other hues. Leaves float lazily, blown hither and thither by the breeze before landing and forming a thick and multi tinged carpet. My eyes are fixed on the phenomenon. Otherwise, October in Ireland is like September in Goa, dripping but not pouring wet. And green fields. The drive keeps reminding me of the landscape I have left behind. A Cross in every corner. A little chapel at every turn. A church in every village. Only the structures are as grey as the sky above not whitewashed as in Goa. And it is St. Patrick instead of St. Francis whose intercession is sought in times of danger and difficulty.

The one stark difference between what I have left behind and where I am now, is the road. It is broad, the drive smooth, and the traffic orderly. Fr. O'Brien gets the driver to halt at a wayside cafe. As we enter Father is warmly greeted by the pretty lady at the counter.

"Time to taste Irish snacks if you desire to be real Irish," speaks Father as the menu is placed before us.

"What is your preference?" no reply from us.

Father says, 'Let me place the order. Alright get us steaming hot cups of Barry's tea, Jacob's cream crackers with butter and Hula hoops" "Make it six cups and make it snappy" he shouts out behind the waiter.

And then he calls back. "Oh I forget, my friends here, are Indians. Perhaps they will enjoy onions. Get two plates of mega meanies too."

Nothing could be more delicious. The mega meanies fit like little rings on the fingers. We gulp down every bit. Father picks up the bill ignoring our protests. "So long as you are under my hospitality I pay. And when I cannot pay, I pray" he says amidst laughter.

"From tomorrow you have to fend for yourselves," he concludes.

We resume our journey.

Tall hedges line the road once we leave Dublin behind and enter the countryside. Grasses grow right on to the edge of the tarred surface of the roads. The environment is dust free.

Narrow and long bricks are stacked in several places. I gather they are peat briquettes cut from the peat bogs and left to dry. It is the principal fuel for cooking and heating in the villages. The terrain is dominated by smooth-sided hills interspersed with lakes, brooks, streams and little waterfalls. The effect is mesmeric. Roadside verges still display remnants of what I visualise must have been a colourful flower paradise weeks earlier before summer cooled into autumn. Tiny white-washed houses, thatched huts, farms carved into the hillsides, desolate farms and abandoned houses evidence a rural hinterland. Like in Goa, haystacks abound. And carts pulled by horses or donkeys bring in nostalgia of ox-yoked carts back in the land we have left behind. After a little more than three hours of a wonderful and scenic drive we arrive before a cozy little pastel-shaded cottage overlooking a little brook.

Father O'Brien as always has taken care of every detail. Not just the visa and job. It was also he who used his contacts to obtain a visa for my mother and my uncle through his own sponsorship. He has arranged an old house, owned by his relatives settled in USA, for us to live in until we can buy or rent our own house.

We stand before the family altar. We place a statuette of St. Francis Xavier carried by us on the altar. Father blesses us and prays. Together, we sing the hymn-Bless this family. And we four also sing the Konkani hymn to St Francis Xavier, to the admiration of Father O'Brien.

Alberto takes out his trumpet, goes out in the front yard, and calmly but vigorously plays the old classic Que Sera, Sera. Two elderly neighbors peep in. Father invites them and introduces us. They are happy to have neighbours from India. And surprised too that we are Catholics. Until they learn that we come from Goa.

Father says he will be back in two days time. He will take me to the college which has offered to employ me as assistant librarian. I am prepared to work hard for my confirmation. Before taking leave he promises to look for a job for my wife too and obtains details about her qualifications. He is quite confident that Alberto will get a job as the choir master at the local parish. That leaves Maria as the house keeper.

As Father O'Brien leaves, he offers to keep some money with us for our daily needs. We thank him but decline the offer. He has done enough for us. We must not burden him more. At any rate, before coming we had converted most of our savings into dollars and British pounds. And that includes a sizeable fortune that Celine inherited. We had managed to get only a few Irish pounds as that currency was not available in India. All these transactions were in the black market at a premium and the currency has been concealed and carried.

It is past six and the sun is hovering just above the horizon. There is a stack of firewood and peat briquettes in the store room. The fireplace too is loaded and just needs the match stick. The fire is lit. It takes a while to spread and warm the room. We have some canned food for dinner, which practice we plan to continue until we can really settle down. The elders retire to their rooms. It is too cold for them. Jetlag is overcome but it may take time to adjust from the heat of the tropics to the cold of the Irish autumn with winter at the doorsteps.

Celine and I continue to relax on the sofa hand in hand wondering over the happenings. There is a feeling of romance as the embers die out forcing us to snuggle even closer. But we feel comfortable in each other's company. The future is ours to build together. Destiny has united us after an amazing journey. I go to sleep, with Celine by my side. The cold makes us hug even closer as we fall into deep sleep.

"Congratulations Ismael, You have followed your dream and achieved your personal legend. And not just you, but Alberto too. And Pobres has met his nemesis. It was a similar dream that sent me chasing my personal legend over the desert sands of North Africa and into Egypt centuries ago. Some day you will appear in a dream to another young man and send him chasing his personal legend. It happens all the time. My name is Santiago."

"Yes. Thank you for sending me on this wonderful journey Santiago. I could not be happier and more fulfilled," I hear myself say.

The journey that began with a dream ends with a dream.

No more is it a long way to Tipperary. Because I actually live there now, with my wife and my mother. (And mother in law!). And Alberto, my uncle. He is happy. He has after a long journey, fraught with pain and suffering, found, what he has been seeking. A shortcut to Tipperary. At last.